Jeffrey Introduces
13 More Southern Ghosts

Jeffrey Introduces 13 More Southern GHOSTS

COMMEMORATIVE EDITION

Kathryn Tucker Windham

With a New Afterword by
Dilcy Windham Hilley and Ben Windham

THE UNIVERSITY OF ALABAMA PRESS
Tuscaloosa

The University of Alabama Press
Tuscaloosa, Alabama 35487-0380
uapress.ua.edu

Hardcover edition published 2015.
Paperback edition published 2021.
eBook edition published 2015.

Inquiries about reproducing material from this work should be
addressed to the University of Alabama Press.

Typeface: Times New Roman

Photographs by Kathryn Tucker Windham (unless otherwise indicated)
Cover and illustrations by Sharon Foster
Layout and design by Vic Grimes

Paperback ISBN: 978-0-8173-6036-8

A previous edition of this book has been cataloged by the Library of Congress.
ISBN: 978-0-8173-1873-4 (cloth)
E-ISBN: 978-0-8173-8845-4

Foreword

When Jeffrey (he is the ghost-in-residence at the Windham household in Selma, Alabama) began clumping up and down the hall, slamming doors, moving furniture, scaring the cat, and rocking in an antique chair, we never imagined that his presence would lead to our introduction to some of the South's most splendid ghosts.

Technically, we never actually met any of Jeffrey's Southern friends of the spirit world, but our interest in Jeffrey (there is absolutely nothing like having a ghost in your own house to arouse interest in the supernatural!) has led us into the fascinating field of ghoulish genealogy.

Having a ghost—and admitting it openly—somehow encourages other people to share similar experiences, to retell some of their own tales of the supernatural. And so our collection of ghost stories grew; our acquaintances among Southern ghosts widened.

No one, not even those returning revenants who appear century after century and thus presumably keep in close touch with developments in the spirit world, could ever know all the ghosts who haunt this land, this South, for an amazing array of spirits dwell here.

There is something about the South that encourages, perhaps even requires, the presence of ghosts and the measured retelling of their deeds. And, somehow, these stories provide a nostalgic link with the past, with generations who were here before.

It was, as we said, because of our association with Jeffrey that we became interested in the ghosts whose stories are recorded here. Each of these stories is representative of similar tales told throughout the South to the gentle rhythm of chairs rocking on a wide porch or recounted around an open log fire on a stormy night.

These tales are told not to frighten or even to raise troubling questions. They are told to help preserve some of the South's heritage of great stories. If a reader should become frightened or uneasy so that sleep does not come easily, there is a simple precaution he can take to ward off evil or unwanted visitations:

> PLACE YOUR SHOES ON THE FLOOR AT THE EDGE OF THE BED WITH ONE TOE POINTING UNDER THE BED AND THE OTHER TOE POINTING IN THE OPPOSITE DIRECTION.

With shoes placed in that position, nothing bad will ever happen. Jeffrey guarantees it!

And now here are some of Jeffrey's cohorts, some Southern ghosts he would like for readers to meet.

Contents

At the edge of the city park in Harrodsburg, Kentucky, a white picket fence encloses a single grave near a spring house out of the misty past.

●●

The Girl Nobody Knew

●●

At the edge of the city park in Harrodsburg, Kentucky, a white picket fence encloses a single grave. The metal marker above the concrete slab is inscribed,

"UNKNOWN—Hallowed and Hushed Be the Place of the Dead. Step Softly . . . Bow Head."

Here is buried a girl, young and beautiful, whose name no one knows, whose story can only be pieced together with sketchy recollections, suppositions, and speculation.

Today the city of Harrodsburg cares for her grave, just as it has for more than one hundred and twenty-five years. And today children playing in the park pause beside the fence, read the flaking inscription and ask, "Whose grave is this? Who is buried here?" just as children for generations have asked. If these inquiring children are persistent in their questioning, this is the story they will hear:

Back during the 1840's, Harrodsburg was famous as a resort for fashionable summer visitors who came to drink the water from its mineral springs. From May until October, hundreds of visitors came to vacation in this middle Kentucky town: some came hoping to be benefited by the waters while others were attracted by the social life—the parties, banquets, plays, horse races, concerts, gambling, dances, and masquerade balls.

On a tree-shaded hill near the edge of town stood an imposing brick hotel, The Harrodsburg Springs Hotel. Dr. and Mrs. C. C. Graham, owners of the establishment, had spent a fortune developing their hotel into one of the finest in the entire country. Winding paths, bordered by shrubs and flowers, led to the mineral springs where guests could sit on curved benches inside the latticed spring houses as they shared conversations and drank the healing waters.

The hotel's ballroom was so large and so elegant and so famous that the simple remark, "I attended the ball at Harrodsburg Springs," was enough to establish a social reputation. The dining room was nationally known for its splendid meals, and service throughout the hostelry was unsurpassed.

But it was its ballroom which brought Harrodsburg Springs Hotel its greatest fame. Even during the daylight hours when the room was quiet and empty, its very size gave visitors a sense of grandeur and awe. And at night, when the mirrored walls reflected the graceful images of the bowing, gliding, whirling dancers, there was not a more colorful spectacle in all Kentucky.

Servants lighted the ballroom's crystal chandeliers and the lamps, more than one hundred of them, each night after supper. Then by the time the guests had changed into their evening finery, the Negro musicians, trained by Dr. Graham and outfitted by him in splendid uniforms, were at their places on the raised platform ready for the dancing to begin.

As the dancers took their places on the ballroom floor (many a romance flowered at Harrodsburg Springs), spectators sat in chairs along the walls or paused in doorways to watch the graceful kaleidoscope of rhythm and, perhaps, to whisper about who was flirting with whom.

It was on such a scene of carefree pleasure that the heroine of Kentucky's story of mystery made her brief appearance.

Her story, as pieced together by recollections of people who were there and then handed down from one generation to the next, began late one summer afternoon, shortly before supper time. Many of the hotel's guests were seated in rocking chairs on the wide gallery exchanging bits of gossip and enjoying the easterly breeze that had just sprung up. They ceased their rocking and their talking when a carriage stopped at the entrance and out of it stepped a girl so lovely that afterwards the people who saw her arrive could never adequately describe her appearance.

"She had a glow about her, an ethereal quality," they would say. Or, "Her hair—it was piled on top of her head, and ringlets hung down around her shoulders, and it glistened with a golden sheen in the late sunlight." Or, "Such a smile she had—a smile of pure joy as though she wanted to share her love of life with everyone she saw."

Later nobody quite agreed on what color her hair really was or what kind of eyes she had or even how tall she was, but they all agreed that she was the loveliest young girl they had ever seen.

They noticed that she arrived alone, which was unusual in those days when ladies never traveled without an escort, and that she had only one piece of luggage, a small trunk which the carriageman took into the hotel before he drove away.

She registered, some observers recalled, as Miss Mary Virginia Stafford of Louisville, and she explained to the desk clerk that her parents, Judge and Mrs. Stafford, would arrive later in the evening. They, she added, would bring the rest of her luggage. She had come early so she would have time to rest before dressing for the ball, she said.

"I love to dance," she confided in a voice so sweet and enticing that a dozen or more young men in the lobby surged around her to beg for the privilege of being her escort for the ball.

She thanked each one graciously but declined their invitations. "I will save a dance for each of you," she promised as she turned from the lobby and went toward her room.

She did not come down to supper, and when she did not appear in the ballroom for the grand march, curiosity about her identity and her actions became intense. Some guests from Louisville stated that they had never seen the young lady at any social functions there, not even at church (they were Episcopalians and thought she had the unmistakable quality look of an Episcopalian), nor had they ever known a Judge Stafford in Louisville. They wondered if - - -

Before the questions grew into insinuations and the insinuations into gossip, Miss Stafford (if indeed that was her name) walked into the ballroom. Walked is hardly the proper word to use, for she seemed to float in, caught up in the happy excitement of the music, the lights, the crowd, and the dancing.

Immediately she was surrounded by young men who reminded her of her promise 'to dance with them, and she danced with partner after partner.

Everyone at the ball watched her, and she was the chief topic of conversation. Even the people who were most skeptical about her background and most envious of her popularity admitted that they had never seen a young lady more beautiful, more graceful, more gracious, or more completely charming than she.

"I don't know whose daughter she is, but I wish she were mine," one matriarch remarked. And all around her heads bobbed in agreement.

13

At intermission the girl, accompanied by a covey of young gallants, strolled out into the summer night. She was silent as they walked through the shadows of the tall trees into splotches of moonlight. It was not the silence of rudeness or of weariness but rather a quietness sometimes induced by those rare times of total happiness when there is no need for words.

The night was heavy with the sweetness of honeysuckle and of late blooming four-o-clocks. Somewhere nearby a mockingbird sang. At the first notes of the bird's clear song, the girl stood still and lifted her hand for silence. As the song ended, she murmured softly,

"Oh, I am so happy! I wish I could stay right here always. Forever and ever - - -"

Then she laughed, caught the hand of the young man nearest her, and urged, "Come on! Let's hurry back to the hotel. I hear the music—I don't want to miss a single dance!"

Her companions recalled that her merriment increased as the night grew longer, and several of her partners heard her exclaim, "I wish the music would never stop, that the dancing could go on and on and on!"

Finally, despite those wishes, the hotel manager announced, "This will be the final dance of the evening. We hope you have had a pleasant time."

The girl glided onto the floor with her final partner. Then as the music neared its end, she suddenly collapsed in the young man's arms.

She was dead.

The death of anyone so young and so lovely would naturally have caused grief, but her sudden passage from life into death had a peculiarly poignant sadness for she, apparently, had no family or friends. The name she had used to register at the hotel was fictitious as was the other information she had provided the desk clerk. Her personal belongings gave no clue as to who she was. Hotel officials hoped to find something in her small trunk to help them establish her identity, but when they forced the lock, they found the trunk empty.

Newspapers carried accounts of the "girl who danced herself to death" and asked the help of readers in learning who she was. Hundreds of people came to Harrodsburg to view the body, still supremely beautiful in death, but no one knew her.

So, despairing of finding her family, guests at the hotel joined with the management in preparing for her funeral. The young men remembered how she had said, "I wish I could stay here always," and they chose as her burial place the spot where she had stood to listen to the mockingbird.

Her dancing partners served as her pallbearers, and the Negro musicians from the hotel played a funeral dirge. Roses twined with honeysuckle covered her casket.

After the funeral, the search continued for someone who knew the girl. Weeks, months, years passed, and her identity remained as deep a mystery as it was the night she died. And now, a century and a quarter later, her remains still lie in a grave marked "UNKNOWN."

The Harrodsburg Springs Hotel burned years ago, leaving few reminders of its former elegance or its historic past. But residents of that Kentucky city still report seeing sometimes, late at night, a young girl in an old-fashioned ball gown wandering around near the hotel site. She seems confused and distressed, people who have encountered her say, and she appears to be trying to talk, but no words are audible.

One of the last reported encounters with the lovely ghost came one night when a nurse, a resident of the area, was taking a midnight walk in the park. Her brother, a deaf mute, was ill, and she had been at his bedside for many hours. Other members of the family helped with the nursing chores, but since she was the only one who had learned to read lips, she was needed almost constantly.

While he was sleeping that night, she slipped out for a peaceful walk in the park. Near the springhouse, she saw a figure in white approaching her. As the figure came closer, she recognized it as the ghost she had heard about so often, the ghost of the "girl who danced herself to death." The figure appeared to be confused and distressed, just as she had heard from others who had encountered the wraith, and seemed to be trying to talk. The nurse stood in the arc of light cast by an overhead street lamp until the figure came close enough for her to read its lips.

"I'm lost. Please help me. I was attending a ball at the hotel, but now I can't find my way back," the figure said, not making a sound.

"My dear," the nurse replied, "the hotel burned more than fifty years ago."

The specter threw her hands over her face and rushed, sobbing, into the springhouse where she vanished completely.

*Here on this track at Surrency, Georgia, when
the train neared his home, Allen Surrency
put away his ledger and looked again
in his brown valise.*

●●

A Ghost Who Threw Things

●●

The train ride from Macon to Surrency, a distance of some one hundred and twenty five miles, had seemed longer than usual to Allen Surrency. He was eager to get back home.

The conductor moved down the aisle of the swaying coach calling, "Baxley! Baxley! Next stop Baxley, Georgia!"

He paused by Allen Surrency's seat and said, "Better warn your cook that I'll be stopping at your place for breakfast day after tomorrow—tell her to cook a big pan of biscuits for me!"

The two men laughed and spent a few minutes talking about cotton and the price of naval stores and politics before the conductor moved on through the train.

Allen Surrency knew all the train crews on the Macon to Brunswick run. His big house in Surrency, the town named for his family, served as a hotel and restaurant for the railroad men and for other visitors, and he had many friends among them.

When the train neared Surrency, Mr. Surrency put away the ledger in which he had been figuring receipts from his sawmill and general store, and he looked again in his brown valise to make sure he had not forgotten the presents for his children. His wife, Welthier, accused him of spoiling the children—and perhaps he did.

The conductor came through the coach again calling, "Surrency! Surrency! Surrency, Georgia!"

Mr. Surrency stood up, brushed the cinders off his coat and trousers and picked up his valise and the bundles he had brought from Macon. He glanced out the window to see which of his children had walked across to the station to meet him—he was almost sure his daughter Clementine would be there—and was surprised to see a large and apparently excited crowd of people gathered along the railroad siding.

"What do you suppose has happened?" he asked the conductor, and together they rushed down the aisle to the exit.

As Mr. Surrency stepped from the train, his storekeeper greeted him with, "Hurry home, Mr. Surrency. Awful things are happening at your house—a ghost has taken over the place!"

Thus Allen Surrency learned of the ghost which was to torment members of his household for more than five years.

At first Mr. Surrency refused to believe the stories neighbors told him as they hurried together across the tracks and through the oak grove to his home. A ghost disrupting his household? Impossible!

Even when his wife, placid Welthier, burst into tears and his children clung to him in fright, he tried to reject the idea that a supernatural being had caused their upset. Surely, he reasoned, there was a logical explanation for the weird events he was hearing about.

He entered his house, still listening in startled disbelief to the tales being told him, to put away a bag of hardware (nails, hinges, bolts, etc.) he had bought in Macon. Then he walked back out on the porch to try to find someone who could give

20

a sensible account of the events that had occurred during his absence. As he stepped onto the porch, the nails, bolts, and hinges that he had just put away showered down upon him and clattered to rest in a circle around his feet.

Allen Surrency never doubted again!

Now, a century after the still unexplained events which bedeviled the Surrency household and which brought thousands of curiosity-seekers to the town, it is difficult to determine just how the strange hauntings began.

Some accounts say Mrs. Surrency, Welthier, was the first member of the family to be annoyed by the supernatural visitor. She was sitting alone in her room, this version says, sewing and planning menus for the next day when her handwork jerked away from her and swirled in circles and arcs around the room.

As she gazed in amazement, her spools of thread, thimble, and scissors leapt from her lap and joined in the aerial acrobatics.

Mrs. Surrency ran from the room in terror. Behind her she heard the noise of shattering china as her bowl and pitcher set jumped from her wash stand and crashed to the floor.

Other accounts say the strangeness began when the Surrencys' daughter, Clementine, was bombarded by a shower of hot bricks as she skipped up the front steps of her home.

Yet another version says the boys in the family were the ghost's first victims. According to this narration, the boys were sitting in the living room talking with a visiting minister (their mother had instructed them to entertain the guest while she finished dressing) when a blazing log flew out of the fireplace and whirled around the room. As if waiting for their cue, the andirons began to do an awkward, noisy dance as the tongs beat a rhythm on the stone hearth.

The minister, it is reported, cut short his visit and rushed off to see other parishioners.

However it began, the weeks and months and years that followed marked a time of terror for Allen Surrency and his family. From 1872 until the ghost departed some five years later, life for the Surrencys was never normal.

The ghost broke everything in the house that was breakable: bowls and pitchers, mirrors, windowpanes, vases, dishes, flower pots, glasses, pictures, jars were all flung upon the floor or against the walls with such force that they shattered into smitherines.

At first Mr. Surrency brought plates and glasses from his general store to replace the broken crockery, but after the breakage continued, the family finally resorted to using tin plates and cups. Yet apparently the ghost enjoyed rattling tin as much as he delighted in crashing china: when the family gathered for a meal, the tin plates swirled off the table and clattered to the floor—or they sailed through a window out into the yard!

Even amidst the turmoil, the cook, Sal, tried to serve her usual good meals to the family, but the ghost would not permit it. Often the fire in the cook stove went out when the food was only half done, the coffee pot cavorted around the kitchen, skillets and pots of food turned upside down on the stove, and pans of hot biscuits whizzed out of the oven and glided onto the porch.

Finally the family gave up trying to have regular meals, and Sal even stopped cooking. For days at a time their menu consisted of cheese and crackers or potted meat from the store. Even this food had to be clutched tightly and eaten quickly to keep the ghost from snatching it away. Mrs. Surrency, who loved pretty things, grieved as her china and glassware, some of which had been wedding gifts, were destroyed.

But Mr. Surrency was more angered than grieved. He was determined to save one fragile possession which he prized greatly: a pair of ornate glass wine decanters given to him by the Savannah Hunt Club. Burying the decanters would be the only way to protect them from the destructive ghost, Mr. Surrency reasoned, so he dug a hole in the back yard and carefully placed the glass treasures in it. He had covered the hole with dirt and was putting his shovel in the tool shed when he heard a peculiar noise behind him. He whirled around in time to see his lovely decanters shoot into the air and crash to the ground in a hundred pieces. The slivers of broken glass sparkled tauntingly in the bright sunlight.

Stories about the Surrency ghost spread throughout Georgia, and the railroads ran excursions from Macon, Atlanta, Brunswick, and other cities to bring curious spectators to the ghost-tormented house. Thousands of people trooped through the home to see the missing windowpanes, the broken mirrors, the displaced furniture, and other evidences of the ghost's mischief.

Some of those visitors even had personal encounters with the ghost: big sticks of wood, coming out of nowhere, landed with a thud at their feet; irons whizzed past their heads; or heavy pieces of furniture toppled over in front of them. Miraculously, no one was ever injured, and the family even managed to joke half-heartedly about the ghost's poor aim.

24

Much of the wood that was thrown at visitors—and at members of the family, too—came from neatly stacked racks alongside the railroad tracks. Engines in those days burned wood instead of coal, and one of Allen Surrency's many enterprises was to supply some of that fuel. He reportedly cancelled his contract with the railroad after the ghost started using the wood for ammunition!

Allen Surrency also supplied some of the crossties used by the railroad, cutting the thick timbers from his own land and finishing them at his sawmill. Surrency, Georgia, was at that time known as the "Crosstie Capital of the World," and Allen Surrency had helped it earn that title.

It was a crosstie from Allen Surrency's mill that played a major role in one of the ghost's most amazing performances. On this occasion, an excursion train had brought scores of passengers from Macon to Surrency to "see" the ghost. The conductor had visited the house many times since it had been haunted, and, not wishing to subject himself to the ghost's antics again, he stayed aboard the train to talk with a friend while the passengers and other crewmen toured the home.

It was a warm Spring day, and the conductor raised the windows in the coach, hoping to lure a breeze in. Then the two men pushed back a seat and sat facing each other beside the open window. They talked not of the ghost but about the progress of Georgia under the administration of Gov. James M. Smith, the state's first Democratic governor since the end of the war.

They had hardly begun their conversation when they glanced out the window and saw a crosstie hovering in the air beside the train. As the men watched, the heavy timber turned, floated through the open window into the coach, paused briefly between them, and then zoomed out the window on the other side of the train and imbedded the front

25

end two feet deep in the ground!

The self-propelled crosstie remained in that position for many months until tourists whittled it away to get slivers for souvenirs.

Always the Surrency family kept hoping that the ghost would go away, would leave them as suddenly as it had arrived. There were brief periods, a week or more at a time, when nothing unusual happened, and the family rejoiced over the respite. The first few times that the household was undisturbed for several days, Mr. Surrency assumed that the poltergeist had departed, and he replaced the broken window-panes and made other repairs in the house.

Unfortunately, the devilish spirit had not gone for good but was apparently only taking a short vacation. No sooner did all the windows have glass in them again than some unseen force raced through the house raising and lowering windows with such vigor that every pane was shattered again!

After two such experiences, separated by several months, Mr. Surrency left the windows open during the warm months and covered the gaping holes with oilcloth to keep out the cold during the winter.

Each time the ghost went away and returned, it seemed more destructive and more vengeful. Finding nothing to break, it would vent its evil energy by unmaking beds, hiding clothes, upsetting furniture, and pulling the cover off the children, particularly off Clementine. She, it seems, was the favorite victim of the ghost's tricks.

Finally the poor girl became so upset (nobody in the family was exactly calm) that Mr. Surrency decided to move the family out into the country some five miles to a rather small house on one of his plantations. The move was uneventful, and for several days the family lived in unaccustomed peace. But then the ghost seemed to have discovered their whereabouts, and once again the routine of broken glassware, flying furniture, and interrupted sleep began. In fact, the ghostly vandalism was more vicious and frightening than ever.

The Surrencys held a hurried family conference and decided to return to their home in town. The ghost returned with them and seemed to take fresh delight in disrupting meals, turning over furniture, opening and closing doors, and hiding objects.

Then one day in 1877 the supernatural happenings in the Surrency household stopped—forever.

There is no trace left of the Surrency home now: a pecan orchard grows along the tracks where the house stood. But out in the cedar-shaded Overstreet Cemetery, some three miles from Surrency on the road (Georgia 121) to Blackshear, there is a stone marker with the inscription "SURRENCY— ALLEN P. (1825–1877) WELTHIER (1833–1899)."

It is a calm, peaceful place.

●●

The Farmer Who Vanished

●●

In the late 1880's there appeared in *The Cincinnati Inquirer* a news story of the disappearance—vanishing would be more accurately descriptive—of David Lang from his home near Gallatin, Tennessee. The story created a sensation at the time, and nowhere was it read with more interest than at Gallatin. Folks there declared it never happened.

But the reputation of *The Inquirer* is so fine, the story it printed was so plausible, so complete with details and so convincing that even today many people believe that David Lang did live in Gallatin and that he disappeared. According to the story in *The Inquirer* and other accounts published through the years, this is what happened:

One warm afternoon in late September (September 23 is the generally accepted date), 1880, Mrs. David Lang was sitting on her front porch watching her two children play in the yard. Sarah, who was about ten, was making a playhouse around the roots of a big oak tree. She had carpeted her "rooms" with clumps of green moss, and she was constructing furniture from acorn cups, twigs, and bark. Her younger brother, George, was building pens to hold the wooden cows and pigs his father had carved for him. The children's play amused her briefly, but Mrs. Lang was impatient for her husband to finish his farm chores and take her to town.

"We'll never get there before the stores close," she complained to nobody in particular. She needed to buy material for a Sunday dress for Sarah (the child was wearing her old Sunday dress to school) and a shirt for George. And they both needed shoes.

Mrs. Lang rose from her chair and walked to the edge of the porch. She was about to call Mr. Lang, although she knew it would make him angry, when he appeared around the corner of the house.

"I'm coming," he informed Mrs. Lang. "I just want to walk down to see about the horses. It won't take long." He took his watch out of the bib of his overalls and looked at it. "We'll get to town in plenty of time," he assured his impatient wife. Lang opened the gate and started across the pasture. The pasture stretched in a gentle slope away from the house. It was a clean, open grassland without trees or bushes.

The farmer had gone only a short distance when a buggy turned in at the road leading up to his house. In the buggy were two businessmen from Gallatin, longtime friends of the family, who had come out to discuss a proposed land sale with Lang. One of the visitors saw Lang starting across the pasture, and he stood up in the buggy to call to him.

"David! Wait!" he shouted.

Mrs. Lang and the children watched as David Lang turned to wave and acknowledge the greeting of his friend.

Then David Lang disappeared. One minute he was standing in his own familiar pasture waving at a friend; the next minute he had disappeared, vanished completely—and forever.

Mrs. Lang ran screaming from the porch out to the

pasture. The children threw down their playthings and followed her. The two visitors jumped from their buggy, climbed the fence, and dashed to the spot where they had last seen Lang.

There was absolutely no sign of him.

The grass, short and dry in the early fall, was crushed down at the spot where David had turned to wave at his friends, and that patch of trampled grass was the only evidence that anyone had been in the pasture. As the startled, almost hysterical people watched, the grass slowly righted itself and stood stiff and tall. Now nothing remained to indicate that, moments before, a man had stood on the spot.

His family and friends began a frantic search for David Lang, but there was nowhere to look. There was no shrubbery or bushes, not even a clump of weeds, that could hide a man in the pasture. There were no wells or sinkholes or crevices in the earth.

Mrs. Lang dropped to her knees and began digging frantically into the earth where she had last seen her husband. The hard ground tore her fingers, and blood mingled with her tears to mark the fateful spot. The visitors finally led her gently back to the house where one of them sat with her and the dazed children while the other one went to fetch help from neighbors.

Neighbors came, many of them, but though they searched every foot of the Langs' farm and of the adjoining farms as well, they found no trace of the missing man. A well-digger brought his rig and began excavating at the spot where Lang disappeared, but he soon struck limestone and had to abandon the effort. Bloodhounds were brought out by the county sheriff. The dogs lost the trail in the open pasture, right where Lang had disappeared. When they reached that spot, they tucked their tails and whined so pitifully that the sheriff ordered them put into the wagon and taken back to town.

Although the search continued for days, not one clue as to Lang's whereabouts was ever found.

At night, every night for two weeks, Mrs. Lang and neighbors at her house (friends arranged to stay with the poor woman twenty-four hours a day—she was in no condition to be left alone) heard David Lang call for help.

"Help me! Please somebody, help me!" they heard Lang begging.

The cries seemed to come from the place where Lang disappeared, but though his family and friends, who did earnestly want to help him, listened hard and looked harder, they never found the source of the cries. Each night the voice became weaker and more faint until it ceased to be heard entirely.

After several nights passed without Lang's voice being heard, Mrs. Lang agreed to have funeral services for her departed (she hesitated to use the word deceased, not being certain that he was) husband. It did not seem proper, somehow, to have a man's funeral while his voice was still audible.

The next spring, when the grass in the pasture came up fresh and green, nature marked the spot of David Lang's mysterious disappearance with a perfect circle of stunted brown grass some fifteen feet in diameter.

Years afterwards, Ambrose Bierce, the American journalist-author who later disappeared as completely and almost as mysteriously as did David Lang, wrote about the Tennessean who vanished. He believed the story. And, though reputable citizens of Gallatin have denied its truth for years, so do a lot of other people.

This is thought to be the field near Gallatin, Tennessee, where David Lang disappeared, although over the decades the grass has grown green and only the shadows suggest a change of texture.

●●

Harpist Of The Gulf

●●

"You're lovely, my dear—even when you're seasick!" Senor Vinesto told his wife. "When we reach New Orleans, you'll be the most beautiful, the most elegant lady there."

Julia Vinesto tried to smile at her husband's flattery, but the rough rolling of the ship made her too miserable to pretend pleasure. She had pretended too long, too many years already. And now she was becoming tangled in the most dangerous pretense of all.

As she tried to straighten out her thoughts, it seemed to Julia that it had been years since she and her husband boarded ship and fled from Uruguay. It was difficult to recall the leisurely, carefree life they had once known at their town house in Montevideo and at their country estate when friends joined them for banquets, parties, and balls.

Now many of those friends were dead, killed in the revolution, while others had escaped across the borders to Argentina or Brazil. Those last days in Uruguay were a blurred nightmare of running, hiding, slipping past armed soldiers, and, finally, finding safety aboard the small ship bound for New Orleans.

How long they had been aboard that ship Julia could not remember. Two weeks? A month? It seemed forever. Grateful as she was for their escape, Julia was tired and bored—bored by the other passengers, bored by the absence of any social life, and, though she shrank from admitting it, bored by her husband.

He, twenty-five years her senior, had always bored her. But he had social prestige, political power—and money, enough of all three to make her quite willing to be his wife. Now only the money was left, a chest of gold Brazilian coins locked in their stateroom.

"Julia, you will be the toast of New Orleans," he had promised her. "We will buy a splendid mansion. With you as hostess, it will be the social center of all Louisiana."

Looking at him now Julia, good Catholic though she was, wondered if divorces were easily obtained in New Orleans.

Captain Hawes, commander of the ship, was wondering about New Orleans divorces, too. From the night he had helped Julia and her husband—how clumsy he was!—climb from their rowboat onto the deck of his ship, he had been in love with Julia. The captain was a perceptive man, and it did not take him long to discover that Julia was lonely, that she longed for the companionship of someone nearer her own age.

So, in a discreet way, he became attentive to her. First there were conversations at meals, after he had invited the couple to share the captain's table. Then there were casual encounters on deck with small talk about weather signs and navigation and foreign ports and such.

Almost before she knew it, Julia had fallen in love with the captain. Then began secret meetings, whispered confidences, and plans for a life shared together somewhere in the United States.

"Don't you worry," the captain assured Julia. "I'll take care of you. We'll make a new life, a happy life together."

But Julia was worried. Her conscience troubled her, and she feared that her husband, a jealous man, would learn of her clandestine meetings with Captain Hawes.

Senor Vinesto did notice a change in his wife, but he attributed her moodiness to homesickness.

"You miss your music, don't you?" he asked one day.

Julia was an accomplished musician and played beautifully on the harp, plucking its strings with rare feeling and skill.

"Yes," Julia replied, "I do miss my music, particularly my harp."

Actually she had not thought of her harp in many, many days, but she hoped her reply would divert any suspicions her husband might have about her unusual behavior.

A few days later, when the ship put into port to take on fresh water and to replenish food supplies, Senor Vinesto sent ashore and purchased a harp. It was not a large or fine instrument, but he hoped it would bring his wife pleasure.

Thus began the daily harp concerts aboard ship. The passengers and crewmen, those who could slip away from their duties, would gather on deck to hear Julia play. She could play any melody she had ever heard, and her listeners delighted in having her play their favorite songs.

As the ship sailed nearer to New Orleans, Captain Hawes became more and more upset over his relationship with Julia and the possible outcome of the affair. He loved Julia, as much as he was capable of loving any woman, but he loved her husband's gold even more. And he was fearful that as long as Senor Vinesto lived, he could have neither Julia nor the gold.

So Captain Hawes began planning to kill Senor Vinesto.

It was the gentleman's habit to take a brisk stroll around the deck late at night, his "constitutional" he called it. Captain Hawes was quite familiar with this habit, and it offered him a fine opportunity to carry out his evil scheme. He would, he decided, hit the old man a stunning blow on the head, throw his body into the sea, and then report having seen him fall overboard—"a most unfortunate and unhappy accident," he would say.

When Captain Hawes disclosed his evil plan to Julia, she was horrified. "Oh, no! Not murder!" she sobbed. "You must not kill him. You must not!"

But Captain Hawes was not moved by her protests. Killing Vinesto was the only way he could be certain of having Julia and the gold. And that chest was very heavy.

So poor Senor Vinesto "fell overboard" one night.

Julia was distraught. She had never intended for her romance with the captain to end with murder. She begged Captain Hawes to seek forgiveness through the Church. There was a priest aboard, and Julia implored the captain to confess his crime to the priest and, through him, seek forgiveness.

But Captain Hawes refused to listen. In fact, Julia's constant insistence that he ask for absolution irritated him and made him uneasy.

His irritation and uneasiness turned to fear, fear that Julia herself would confess to the priest the true account of Senor Vinesto's death or that she would tell the story to authorities in New Orleans when they reached port. Then the chest of gold—that precious gold—would never be his.

Lust for the gold drove Captain Hawes to begin carrying out another evil scheme. As the vessel neared the southern coastline of the United States, Captain Hawes changed course. He made not for New Orleans but for the small coastal village of Pass Christian, Mississippi.

A night or so later, residents of Pass Christian saw a glare in the Gulf not far off shore, and they knew a ship was ablaze there. The men of the village hurried to their boats and rowed rapidly out toward the burning vessel to try to rescue passengers and crewmen. As they drew near, they heard above the noise of the waves the hauntingly beautiful sound of a harp playing old Portugese love songs—and an Ave Maria.

Before the rescuers could reach the ship, a terrific explosion shattered the hull and hurled burning debris across the churning waves. The would-be rescuers returned to shore, saddened by the loss of life in the tragedy, and puzzled by the plaintive music they had heard.

Next morning, early risers at Pass Christian were surprised to meet on the beach the captain and four crewmen from the ill-fated ship. The captain introduced himself and told an exciting tale of how he and his crewmen had managed to escape from the burning ship—after, of course, they had made every possible effort to save the passengers and other members of the crew.

He did not mention the chest of gold they had brought ashore and buried beneath a giant water oak near the beach. And he pretended great puzzlement when asked about the strange harp music heard on the burning ship.

The captain bought a house facing the Gulf, a rambling place with a wide verandah, and let it be known that he intended to live in Pass Christian permanently. It was rumored that he paid for his house with gold Brazilian coins. The captain, handsome and obviously wealthy, became one of the most popular men in the area, and no social event was complete without the charming fellow's presence.

For a year things went well for Captain Hawes. Then one of his crewmen fell ill with yellow fever. The local doctor did all he could to save the man, but after a few days of intense suffering the seaman died. In his final hours before death came, the man, summoning the last of his ebbing strength, confessed to the doctor the story of murder and intrigue which had brought Captain Hawes and his companions to Pass Christian.

In faltering whispers, the man told of the murder of Senor Vinesto, of the theft of his gold, of the firing of the ship, of the escape of Captain Hawes and his trusted crewmen, and even of Julia's final harp concert.

"When she knew she was going to be left to die on the burning ship, she brought her harp from her cabin and sat on deck playing the songs that had delighted her dead husband," the crewman said.

"We heard those melodies as we left the ship, and, borne by the mists and the winds, they followed us all the way to shore.

"I can hear the music now - - -"

And he died.

The doctor was shocked by the story the dying man told, and, though he had no proof, he was inclined to believe it. He shared the details with only three trusted friends, but somehow the feeling spread through the community that Captain Hawes was involved in some terrible scandal.

When he gave his next big party, nobody came.

The captain, naturally, was alarmed over his neighbors' sudden change of attitude, and he suspected that the dead crewman had disclosed his secret. Frightened now, he began making hasty preparations to escape with his treasure. Late that night, he went to the spot where the chest of gold was buried, and he began digging.

Hidden in the thick shadows of the trees were the doctor and his three friends, watching Captain Hawes' every move. As they watched, they became conscious of a strange sound coming from the calm waters of the Gulf. They heard the unmistakable squeak of rusty oarlocks and the rhythmic

41

swish of oars. And above the sound of the oars came the plaintive strains of harp music.

Captain Hawes heard the rowing and the music, too, and he dug frantically until he wrested the chest from the sand and forced it open.

The sounds were louder now and quite close by. Peering from their dark hiding places, the doctor and his companions saw a battered rowboat approach the shore. At the oars were four skeletons, and seated in the bow, playing on a golden harp, was a beautiful young woman with long black hair blowing in the Gulf breeze.

Captain Hawes looked up and saw the ghostly crew and the sweet harpist. He fell forward, striking his head on the edge of the metal chest.

When the doctor reached him, the captain was dead. In one hand he clutched a few gold coins. The chest was empty.

The phantom lifeboat, the rowers, and the harpist had disappeared, lost in the fog rolling in from the Gulf.

All this happened a long time ago, back in the early 1850's, but people living along the coast near Pass Christian still occasionally report seeing late at night a mysterious glow out in the Gulf, like the glow from a burning ship. And always when they see the glow, they hear strange music, sad snatches of song played softly on a stringed instrument.

Mississippi

At this spot, outside Pass Christian, Mississippi, the "harpist of the Gulf" is said to play her music eternally.

About fifteen miles north of Jackson, Mississippi, near the community of Mansdale, is a lovely Gothic chapel, the Episcopal Chapel of the Cross.

●●

Ghosts Of Annandale

●●

About fifteen miles north of Jackson, Mississippi, near the community of Mansdale, is a lovely Gothic chapel, the Episcopal Chapel of the Cross. It sits on a knoll, some distance back from the road, almost hidden in a grove of oaks, magnolias, and dogwood trees.

The shady grove extends back of the church to a small cemetery where Henry Vick, hero of one of Mississippi's most romantic and most tragic love stories, is buried. It is to this cemetery that the ghost of Vick's sweetheart, the beautiful Helen Johnstone, still comes to grieve over the loss of her lover just as, in life, she came during those sad weeks and months following his death on May 17, 1859.

The story of Helen Johnstone and Henry Vick began during the Christmas holidays in 1855. Sixteen-year-old Helen and her mother, Mrs. Margaret Johnstone, were spending the holidays with Helen's sister, Mrs. William Britton, at Ingleside, the home John Johnstone had built as a wedding gift for his oldest daughter.

Johnstone had laughingly told his wife that he practiced on Ingleside so he would know exactly how to build Annandale, the grand house he planned for his own family to have.

His plans for building this mansion, which he intended to pattern after his family estate—Annandale—in Scotland, were delayed by his wife's insistence that they first build a chapel.

Before construction on the chapel had begun, Mr. Johnstone died, but Mrs. Johnstone went ahead with the project—after a proper period of mourning, of course. She supervised the cutting of timber for the heavy sills and curved rafters, and she made sure that the hand-shaped brick were properly fired in the plantation kiln. It was she who directed the uncrating and the installation of the stained glass windows and the baptismal font from France and of the pews, the altar, the chancel rail, and the pump organ from England.

After the chapel was properly consecrated in 1852, it was Mrs. Johnstone who arranged the ceremony for moving her late husband's body from its temporary burial place in the family flower garden to the graveyard at the rear of the chapel.

Three years later, Mrs. Johnstone began carrying out her husband's plans for Annandale. Work on the house, which was to be more than four years in the building, had just begun that Christmas, 1855, when Mrs. Johnstone and Helen went to nearby Ingleside to spend the holidays.

They were seated at supper there one night when heavy knocking on the front door announced the arrival of an unexpected guest. The servant who answered the knock returned to the dining room to report that a young man from Vicksburg wished to speak with the man of the house, William Britton. The young man, splattered with red mud, was Henry Vick, who was there to ask help in getting his carriage unmired and repaired.

Mr. Britton promised to have men from his plantation get the carriage out of the mud and make the needed repairs. Meantime, he invited Henry Vick to be a guest at Ingleside

46

until he could continue his journey. Before that visit ended (the repairs to the carriage required several days to complete), Vick was deeply in love with Helen Johnstone. Helen, a beautiful girl with light brown hair and blue-grey eyes, had fallen just as deeply in love with him. In fact, Vick had charmed the entire family.

Although Mrs. Johnstone approved of Vick (his family background was quite acceptable, and he himself was obviously a young man who would make his mark in the world), she felt that Helen, barely sixteen, was too young for marriage. So Vick agreed to wait for Helen to "grow up," and for more than three years the couple had a tender, happy courtship.

Vick came often to the Johnstones' home to visit during those years. He watched Annandale grow, and, when asked, he gave Mrs. Johnstone advice or suggestions on problems of construction. On Sunday mornings he and Helen attended services at the Chapel of the Cross, and on Sunday afternoons they watched and listened as Mrs. Johnstone led the slaves, all of them singing, through the woods to the chapel for worship.

As the couple's romance deepened and as the grand house neared completion, Mrs. Johnstone gave her consent for them to set a date for their wedding. They chose May 21, 1859, to be the day of their marriage in the Chapel of the Cross. The reception, to which the whole countryside was invited, was to be held at Annandale.

About a week before the wedding, Vick boarded a river steamer in Vicksburg for a trip to New Orleans to buy wedding clothes for himself and some pieces of furniture for his new home. Soon after his arrival in New Orleans, Vick stopped in a billiard room where he had a chance meeting with James Stith, a former friend with whom he had quarreled months before. As Vick entered that billiard room,

Stith, who had just ordered a drink, threw his glass on the floor and shouted, "I refuse to drink with you, sir! You are no gentleman!"

Vick lunged at Stith, and Stith swung at Vick. Weapons were being reached for when companions separated the pair, but Vick, angry over Stith's public insult, challenged him to a duel, and the challenge was accepted.

A few hours later, Vick regretted his hasty action. He recalled with haunting clarity his promise made to Helen Johnstone that he would never kill a man in a duel. At the time he made the promise, the possibility of his becoming involved in an illegal affair of honor seemed so remote that he gave the pledge easily. He had even laughed at what he termed Helen's "foolish concern" over his dueling. Tortured by the memory of that promise, Vick sent one of his seconds, a Colonel Lockridge, to explain the circumstances to Stith and to ask that the duel be called off.

"Tell that coward I'll hound him like a dog the rest of his days if he refuses to meet me in this duel," was Stith's reply.

Vick then had no choice but to fight.

The men's seconds, Tom Morgan and Frank Cheatham of Baton Rouge for Stith and Colonel Lockridge and A. G. Dickinson for Vick, agreed that Alabama would be the safest place for the duel to be staged. The six of them took the next mail boat from New Orleans to Mobile.

Somehow police in Mobile had learned of the plans for the duel, and they were determined to prevent it from taking place in their city. With the police on the alert for them, the duelists had to move rapidly to escape arrest.

The scene of the duel, one of the last to be fought in Mobile, was probably a grove of trees on Scott Street just north of Charleston, a place known as Holly's Garden. The weapons were Kentucky rifles at thirty paces.

Vick was an excellent marksman (he could kill a running deer with a single shot), but, remembering his promise to Helen, he deliberately shot over Stith's head, and his bullet buried itself in a tree.

Stith shot Vick in the forehead, killing him instantly.

Stith and his seconds left the dueling ground immediately and escaped to New Orleans on the returning mail boat, but Lockridge and Dickinson were delayed by having to make arrangements for an undertaker to come for the body of their dead friend. Before they could slip out of the city, the Mobile police were closing in on them. The two men found refuge in the home of a Mobile physician where they were safe from the citywide police search. However, Dickinson was deeply troubled over the knowledge that his friend's body was lying unattended at the morgue. His concern for the dead Vick prompted him to send a message to the city's chief of police, Harry Maury, confessing his part in the duel and asking that he be permitted to accompany Vick's body back to Vicksburg.

Chief Maury was impressed by Dickinson's honesty and by his loyalty to his friend, so impressed that he helped Dickinson disguise himself for a trip to the morgue. When arrangements were completed there, Chief Maury sent his own carriage to take Lockridge and Dickinson to the mail boat where he himself smuggled them aboard, putting them into a stateroom and locking the door so that police could not search the room.

When they reached New Orleans, Lockridge and Dickinson put Vick's body aboard a packet bound for Vicksburg. On that same packet were the caterer, the cooks, and the helpers on their way to Annandale with materials for the wedding feast. And so Vick's coffin and the trappings for his wedding were taken off the boat at Vicksburg at the same time.

Messengers were sent at once to Annandale to take the sad news to Helen and her family. Helen was helping decorate the chapel, putting magnolia blossoms and greenery in big urns, when her mother came to tell her that Henry Vick was dead. Before she regained her composure, Helen sobbed, "He must be buried here. Henry loved this chapel."

Plans were quickly made to bring Vick's body from Vicksburg to Annandale for burial. It was after dark when the funeral party reached Annandale. The road to the chapel was lighted by flaming torches held by slaves from the Johnstone plantation, and, after the brief services there, their torches outlined the path to the open grave in the cemetery.

Henry Vicks' grave at Annandale

Helen marked the grave, later, with a granite cross inscribed simply, "Henry Grey Vick—Entered Into Rest May 17, 1859." She also had small statues of Vick's hunting dogs placed at the grave.

And day after day Helen sat on an iron bench beside the grave as she wept for her beloved Henry. When twilight came, some member of the family would lead her gently home, but early morning would find her at her vigil again. And over and over she said to her family, "Remember that I am to be buried beside Henry. Please promise me that the grave space next to his will be saved for me and that nobody else will ever be buried there. Promise." And they did.

Finally Mrs. Johnstone, fearing that Helen would grieve herself to death, took the young girl to Europe to help heal her broken heart. They were away for several months, and the change of scene was helpful. When they returned home, Helen had recovered from her deep depression.

She later married the Reverend George Harris (she is said to have told him quite honestly that she could never love him as she had loved Henry Vick), and they moved to the northern part of the state where Helen died in 1916.

The space beside Henry Vick's grave at the Chapel of the Cross is still vacant, but the sorrowing ghost of Helen Johnstone Harris comes there often to brush the fallen leaves from the grave, to run her fingers over the granite letters that spell his name, and to weep.

Many visitors to the secluded cemetery have told of seeing through the trees the figure of a young woman bowed in grief beside a grave. When they get near enough to speak to her, they say, she gives them a startled look and vanishes.

The marker at the grave where the apparition is seen—and where she disappears—reads, "Henry Vick—Entered Into Rest May 17, 1859."

And many people wonder if the space beside his grave is empty after all.

Somehow the history of Annandale is incomplete, unfinished, without the story of Annie Devlin, for she was a part of that great house too. The romantic accounts of the young love which was ended by a tragic duel have overshadowed the story of Annie Devlin so that the little hunchbacked Irish governess has almost been forgotten. But it was Annie Devlin who vowed, "I'll never leave Annandale," and whose spirit haunted that Mississippi mansion until the night it burned to the ground.

On that September night in 1924 when flames destroyed Annandale, it was Miss Devlin, dead for many years, who appeared at an upper window of the home. As she stood at that window with her features clearly illuminated by the fire, spectators on the lawn looked up and gasped in startled amazement. "Look! It's Annie Devlin at the window! She said she would never leave Annandale!"

The appearance of the ghost of Annie Devlin at the fire that night created almost as much excitement as did the fiery destruction of the fine house.

In her lifetime, Annie Devlin was never the center of attention, tending rather to be a greyish part of the background. She was quiet and somewhat retiring and would have been thoroughly nondescript except for her deformity. People noticed her, as they always notice cripples, but their only reaction was likely to be a hasty, "Poor thing!" as they averted their glances and concentrated on more pleasant things.

Miss Devlin tried to make her hunched back less conspicuous by wearing a three-cornered shawl winter and summer, no matter how hot the weather was. Eventually nobody thought of Miss Devlin without immediately thinking of a shawl. As a result, on those gift-giving occasions, Christmas and birthdays and such, she was usually given a shawl.

"Miss Devlin? Oh, let's give her a nice shawl," her employees would say, not recalling that the governess had been given a nice shawl for the past dozen or more Christmases.

While her collection of shawls grew, nobody noticed that she nearly always wore the same woolen triangle around her stooped shoulders. It was a Scotch plaid, the colors of Annandale, given to her by John Johnstone, the Scotsman who brought her to Annandale to tutor his children.

Exactly when she came to Mississippi is not known. In fact, little is known about her beyond her devotion to the Johnstone family and her determination to remain always at Annandale. She probably came to Mississippi soon after Johnstone moved his family from North Carolina to Madison County. The family at that time lived in a log house, large and comfortable but not the elegant dwelling John Johnstone planned to build. He had already selected the site, a wooded elevation, on which he intended to build a replica of his boyhood home in Scotland—Annandale.

Often the family, accompanied by Miss Devlin, walked to the site and talked about the house as John Johnstone drew in the dirt a rough outline of its big rooms. And they all laughed as he picked up Helen, the younger daughter, and tossed her into the air "as high as the white columns will be."

Miss Devlin, though of course she did not say so, was as impatient as was Mr. Johnstone to begin work on Annandale. However, it seems that she was not with the Johnstone family during the building of the house but had accepted a position elsewhere. Thus she not only missed watching the great house rise on the Mississippi hill, she also missed the happiness and the tragedy of Helen Johnstone's love affair with Henry Vick. She had infrequent letters from Helen during the years, but it was not until Helen and Mrs. Johnstone were returning from their European tour (the trip they took shortly after Henry

54

Vick's death) that Miss Devlin saw any member of the family. The three of them, Mrs. Johnstone, Helen, and Miss Devlin, met quite by chance in Tennessee as the Johnstones were on their way home. It was a happy reunion, especially for Miss Devlin.

"Please, Mother, let's take Miss Devlin home with us," Helen urged. "She has never seen Annandale."

So Mrs. Johnstone invited Miss Devlin to come with them to Annandale, and she accepted without hesitation. She had never really been happy since she left the Johnstones, and her greatest wish was to see Annandale. She had dreamed of the house a thousand nights.

Her visit stretched into weeks, and the weeks became months. Although the Johnstones were cordial and polite, Miss Devlin slowly became obsessed with the fear that they would some day ask her to leave. The fact that she had nowhere to go, no family to go to, did not trouble her nearly so much as the thought of leaving Annandale. She loved the house. In its spacious rooms she felt a sense of belonging and of wholeness she had never known before. At times she forgot that she was a lonely, homeless hunchback and became, in her imagination, the mistress of Annandale.

"I can never leave. I won't leave Annandale," she said to herself. When guests, trying to make casual conversation, asked her how long she intended to stay, she would pull her shawl close about her and reply, half laughing so that the questioners never quite knew how serious she was, "Oh, I'll never leave Annandale!"

And each time anyone mentioned her leaving, Miss Devlin became more upset and more determined to stay forever at Annandale.

One night when a servant went to call Miss Devlin to supper, there was no answer to the knock on the door. Even repeated knockings and insistent callings brought no response.

Finally the door was forced open. There on the bed, her plaid shawl draped around her shoulders, lay Annie Devlin. The doctor said she died of an overdose of laudanum.

It was not long after Miss Devlin's death that guests at Annandale began telling of seeing a woman on the stairs or of meeting her in an upstairs hallway.

"She was a little woman—sort of wispy—and she had a plaid shawl around her shoulders," they would say.

Or, "There was a little woman, deformed in some way, in the hall outside my room. I spoke to her, but she didn't reply, just clutched her shawl and went into a bedroom down the hall. I didn't hear the door open or close—strange—but she must have gone into the room. She disappeared. Who was she?"

Members of the family who heard the stories replied, "It was Annie you met, Annie Devlin. She has been dead for some time."

Although most of her appearances were brief and calm, the ghostly figure did occasionally manifest a fiercely possessive attitude about her old room. Once during the Christmas holidays, when the big house was filled with company, a male guest was put in Miss Devlin's room. Some time after midnight, a wakeful host heard the man tiptoe from his room and down the stairs and heard his footsteps cross the yard toward the stables. The host threw a coat over his nightshirt and hurried out to see why his guest was sneaking away in the middle of the night.

"I can't stay in that room," the frightened man said. He brought his horse out of the stall and added, "Somebody—something I can't see—kept pulling the cover off me. No matter how hard I tried, I couldn't hold the cover on my bed. I'll never stay in that room again!"

The host with a promise of finding him other sleeping quarters persuaded the man to return to the house. But never again, the story goes, was a guest ever put in Annie Devlin's room.

It was at the window of this room that Miss Devlin appeared on the night of the fire, the night that Annandale

died. One of the men fighting the blaze looked up at the window and shouted the alarm, "There's still somebody in the house!"

Mrs. Fannie Thompson, custodian of the Chapel of the Cross, looked where the fireman was pointing and recognized Annie Devlin at once. "It's a ghost you're seeing, the ghost of Annie Devlin," she told the fire fighter. Together they and other spectators watched as the bent little woman stood motionless and serene with her familiar three-cornered shawl, the shawl made of Annandale plaid, draped around her shoulders.

Annie Devlin never left Annandale, not as long as the great house stood.

Colonel Marti marveled at the fort's high, thick walls and its intricate labyrinth of underground rooms and passageways. (Photograph courtesy of Flordia Development Commission)

●●●

A Glow In The Dungeon

●●●

Spanish Colonel Garcia Marti and his wife, Dolores, had arrived in St. Augustine in July, 1784, not long after England had ceded the Floridas back to Spain.

Colonel Marti was not happy with his new assignment, considering it unworthy of a man with his military background. St. Augustine was an isolated military post, heavily dependent on outside sources for even its most basic supplies, and the disgruntled colonel felt the city—if such it could be called—was hardly worth defending.

His wife, considerably younger than her brusk husband, was not happy either. The mosquitoes were terrible, the threat of fever was constant, wild savages roamed the woods and swamps within sight of the city—and there was no place to shop! Dolores was thankful that she had brought with her a large wardrobe of fashionable clothes, and she was particularly pleased to have a supply of her favorite perfume, an unusual scent she always wore.

The one thing that interested Colonel Marti at his new post was Castillo de San Marcos, the massive fortress which since the late 1600's had defended St. Augustine. He marveled at the fort's high, thick walls and its intricate labyrinth of underground rooms and passageways.

"Look, my dear," he said to his wife as he took her on a tour of the fortification, "did you ever see such expert stonework? Just look at those walls—thirty feet high and sixteen feet thick! Splendid!"

But Dolores was not at all interested in the walls of an old fort. When, continuing their tour, Colonel Marti led her down the dark steps to the dungeons, she clung to his arm and urged,

"Please, Garcia, let's not go in there. It's too dark and gloomy, I'm frightened!"

The colonel laughed, but he humored his wife, as he usually did, and escorted her up the steps and into the sunlight of the courtyard.

Standing in that courtyard was Captain Manuel Abela, the colonel's assistant.

The colonel did not particularly like Captain Abela (he considered him something of an opportunist—and, also, he instinctively distrusted any man as handsome as the captain), but he did call the young officer over to introduce him to his wife.

Dolores was still trembling, even in the hot Florida sun, from her glimpse of the dungeons, but when she tried to explain her depressed feeling of danger and foreboding, the two men laughed at her. At the sound of his mirth, Dolores looked straight at Captain Abela for the first time. There was something about his laughter that attracted her: it had nothing of the taunting, humiliating ring of Colonel Marti's laughter but had instead a note of sympathetic understanding. His dark eyes reflected that same compassion. Dolores looked away quickly. Her busband was a very jealous man, and she did not wish to do anything, not even return an innocent smile, which would provoke him.

Colonel Marti, however, appeared not to have noticed the quick exchange of glances.

"Captain Abela," he said. "I had wanted to show my wife the view of the sea from the turret, but I must complete my reports to send to officials in Cuba. The boat sails tonight. Please escort Senora Marti to the tower and show her the other unusual features of the fortress. Perhaps you can stir her interest in Castillo de San Marcos more than I have been able to."

Then the colonel went to his headquarters, leaving Dolores and Captain Abela to explore the old fort together.

Colonel Marti's motives are not clear. Perhaps he really did want to complete his reports, but there have been suggestions that he wanted to test his beautiful wife's fidelity.

61

The captain and the colonel's lady dutifully climbed the tower to look at the sea, just as they had been instructed. Then they leaned against the parapet and looked at each other, without any instructions at all. They did not speak for several minutes. Then Captain Abela asked softly,

"Are you happy here in St. Augustine?"

"No," replied Dolores. "Are you?"

"Now I am," he responded as he took her hand and kissed it.

So that is how it started, that clandestine romance between Senora Dolores Marti and Captain Manuel Abela.

During the weeks that followed, they met often, always fearful that they would be discovered. When she could, Dolores slipped out during the early afternoon, the time of siesta when the narrow streets were deserted, and joined Manuel in the yawning shadows of an empty house or in a grove of orange trees along the river. Often from behind shuttered windows amused eyes watched the pair hurrying to their rendezvous, but nobody told Colonel Marti about the meetings. The colonel was not a very popular man in St. Augustine.

During those first months in St. Augustine, Colonel Marti was unusually busy. He was not familiar with the defenses of the city and, though he resented being sent to the remote command, his pride in his military profession demanded that he perform his duties well. It irritated him that the junior officers on his staff did not share his dedication to duty. They, he soon discovered, were more interested in gambling, cock fighting, drinking, and women than they were in mapping military maneuvers or inspecting gun emplacements. In an effort to bring about stricter military discipline among the men, Colonel Marti summoned Captain Abela to a conference on the matter.

Colonel Marti was unusally busy with the defenses of St. Augustine.
(Photograph courtesy of Florida Development Commission)

Now it happened that the captain had just returned to his quarters from a meeting with Dolores when the soldier arrived with Colonel Marti's message.

"How fortunate," he thought to himself, "that I was back in my quarters before the messenger arrived." And he hurried to the colonel's office.

Their conference would likely have been entirely routine had not Colonel Marti asked the captain's help in interpreting some maps which the British had left behind. The maps were spread out on the colonel's desk, and the two men leaned over them to try to decipher the English notations on the margins. The colonel was distracted by something he could not at first define.

"Do you notice anything unusual here?" he finally asked Captain Abela.

The captain, puzzled, shook his head.

"There's something vaguely familiar that is out of place here. It's rather elusive, a fragrance perhaps that I never noticed here before," the colonel continued, and he glanced about the room.

"It could be the scent of orange blossoms," the captain suggested. "The trees are in full bloom now, and I have heard that at times their sweetness is smelled by sailors far out at sea."

"No," replied the colonel, "it is not orange blossoms." He stared hard at Captain Abela before he said slowly,

"It is my wife's perfume."

64

Several days later, after Captain Abela had failed to answer muster and after he had been missing from his quarters for almost a week, Colonel Marti announced that the young officer had been sent to Cuba on a secret mission. And when neighbors inquired about Senora Marti, the colonel informed them curtly that she had become ill and that he had sent her to Mexico to stay with an aunt until arrangements could be made for her return to Spain.

Neither the captain nor Dolores was ever seen again in St. Augustine, and after a while people stopped asking about them.

It was years later, on July 21, 1833, that the end of their story became known. On that date while United States engineer Lieutenant Stephen Tuttle was exploring the dungeons beneath Castillo de San Marcos (there was little else to do, and he was bored), he found a section of wall which, when tapped, sounded hollow.

The solider used his bayonet to chip away the mortar until he could remove some of the stones from the wall. Then, holding a lantern high, he peered into the opening he had made. The lantern illuminated two skeletons chained to the wall! Had he discovered all that remained of Senora Dolores Marti and Captain Manuel Abela? Had Colonel Marti chained them to the wall of the dungeon, the dungeon Dolores had so feared, and sealed them alive behind a thick wall of coquina?

The soldier who opened the ghastly tomb told later of the sweet, subtle fragrance that filled the underground passageway when he removed the blocks.

Now people who visit the ancient fortress say there is sometimes a strange glow in the shadowy darkness at the spot where the lovers died. And when that glow is seen, a sweet fragrance, like the fragrance of a lady's fine perfume, floats on the dank air of the dungeon of Castello de San Marcos.

Because these lucky dogs have never hunted in the haunted hunting grounds at Sewell's Woods, they were able to pose for the above photograph peacefully.

●●

Disappearing Hounds

●●

"Possum up the 'simmon tree,
    Raccoon on the ground.
    Raccoon say to the possum,
    'Shake them 'simmons down.' "

The possum, that ugly, bare-tailed, marsupial inhabitant
of Southern woods has long been immortalized in folk tales
and songs. Uncle Remus, creation of Joel Chandler Harris,
told tales about Br'er Possum, even a tale about how he
happened to lose the hair on his tail. The expression "playing
possum" has become a part of the American language, and
recipes for cooking possum are included in many cookbooks.

But though he is celebrated in song and story, though his
protective trick of playing dead has added color to the
language, and though roast possum is considered a delicacy by
some diners, old Br'er Possum's greatest contribution to his
native South is the recreation he provides possum hunters.

Back in 1920 there was not a more enthusiastic possum
hunter in Marietta, Georgia, than David Perkins. He was a
husky young fellow, and staying up all night and following
hounds over half a county did not wear him out—he would be

67

on his job on time the next day, alert and ready to work. And he would be raring to go possum hunting again the next time anybody suggested such an outing.

One night Perkins and some hunting cronies were sitting around a fire in the woods warming while they listened to their dogs trying to pick up a fresh possum trail when one of the men began telling of a strange experience he had while hunting. Such tale-telling is one of the pleasures of possum hunting. According to the man's story, he and his companions heard their dogs give the whining barks that signaled they had treed a possum. Before the men could get to the scene, they heard the dogs yelping and howling in a terrible way. In a few minutes the hunters saw their hounds race in terror down a hill and into a gentle valley.

Those dogs were never seen again, the story teller said. He was about to add some details when Perkins heard his lead dog yelp in the way that meant he was hot on the trail of a possum. All the men jumped up to listen to the chase, and the story of the lost hounds was temporarily forgotten.

Later, however, during the ride back home, Perkins asked for more information about the puzzling disappearance of the hounds. He, quite frankly, could not believe such a thing had really happened—dogs do not just disappear. However, his friend told such a convincing story that, despite his disbelief, he determined to see for himself if it could be true.

So Perkins gathered up some cooperative friends (he warned them that they ran the risk of losing their hounds), and they went to what became known as the "haunted hunting grounds." The place was Sewell's woods, located some fifteen miles from Marietta.

It was not yet dark when the hunters arrived, so they got their dogs out of the truck and put them on leashes until darkness came. As soon as the dogs were turned loose, they picked up the scent of a possum. The pack yapped and bayed, sharp and eager, back and forth in a little valley, and then they took off up the side of a high hill. On top of that hill they treed, and they broadcast their success by whining and baying real slowly.

Before the hunters could get up the hill to capture the possum, those dogs started a terrible commotion, yelping and squalling as though somebody was beating them. They ran at full speed, the whole pack of them down the hill, still barking and howling in an unnatural way. The hounds passed within fifty feet of their owners, who whistled and shouted, but they did not even slow down.

Not one of those hounds ever came home. Perkins and his friends advertised in the paper and they notified other hunters to be on the lookout for the missing dogs, but the animals were never heard from again.

Not everybody believed the story about the disappearing dogs. Finally Perkins got tired of being accused of lying, even in a teasing way, so he invited a group of the doubters to bring themselves and their hounds to a hunt in Sewell's woods. That hunt was almost an exact duplicate of the earlier one: the dogs struck the trail, followed it up the same hill, were seized with a frenzy of barking, and came tearing down the hill as though being chased by devils.

Nobody ever saw them again.

By that time half of Marietta was talking about the possum hunts in Sewell's woods and speculating about what happened to the dogs. Nobody was more puzzled than David Perkins himself.

"There's something strange, mighty strange, going on up that hill," Perkins reasoned. He determined to inspect that hilltop—if he could find somebody to go up there with him. Perkins talked his plan over with several folks, but, though they wanted to have the mystery solved, they were not interested in doing any exploring on top of that hill.

69

Finally a fellow named Tom, a young daredevil who was not afraid of anything, agreed to go with Perkins. Their plan was to climb the hill before the hunt started and be there when the dogs arrived. That way, they figured, they would be able to see what it was that bewitched the dogs.

So Tom, Perkins, and several other hunters took a pack of hounds out to Sewell's woods late one afternoon. Tom and Perkins left their hunting companions with the dogs, and they set out up the hill. The dogs were to be released after dark, giving Perkins and Tom plenty of time to get settled on the hill. It was a steeper climb than they had expected, and when Tom and Perkins reached the top they were breathing hard and were hot despite the twilight chill. After they caught their breath, they pushed through mounds of dead blackberry vines and thick underbrush until they came to a small clearing.

In the clearing was a cemetery, a family burial ground. It had been long neglected. Many of the graves had fallen in, and tombstones had toppled over. Tall weeds and bushes, killed by the early frost, stood like grey sentinels posted to discourage intruders.

Tom and Perkins were a little uneasy, but they made some feeble jokes as they selected a vantage spot from which to watch the arrival of the dogs.

Not long after dark, they heard the hounds baying down in the low lands, and it was not long before the pack was heading up the hill. Perkins saw the dogs, eager and excited, lope over the crest of the hill and run into the cemetery. The hounds stopped not twenty-five feet from where Tom and Perkins were standing. The dogs, all of them, began jumping around and whining as though they had treed a big possum, and they seemed to be looking up in a tall tree at their prey.

But there was no tree.

Then, all at once, the dogs fell over backwards. As soon as they scrambled to their feet, they shook themselves and sort of jumped around and then set up a wild chorus of barking as they raced full speed down the hill. Perkins and Tom whistled and shouted and even blew an old hunting horn, but the dogs paid them no attention.

Those dogs never stopped barking and never stopped running from whatever it was that had terrified them up on that hill in Sewell's woods. Maybe they ran themselves to death. Nobody ever saw them again.

David Perkins lives in Anniston, Alabama, now, across the line from Georgia. He no longer hunts in Sewell's woods. And though he has puzzled over the experiences for half a century, he still has no explanation for the "Mystery of the Disappearing Hounds."

Here are some of the acres on the Bell property in Robinson County, Tennessee, where Kate the witch had her fun.

Our Family Trouble

"Oh, grave, where is thy victory? Oh, death, where is thy sting?" intoned the Rev. Sugg Fort as he ended the graveside funeral services for John Bell. Several men, friends of John Bell, stepped forward and began shoveling dirt to fill the grave as the other mourners walked slowly away from the scene.

Suddenly a loud, raucous voice began singing, "Row me up some brandy, Oh! Row me up some brandy!" It was hardly a proper song to sing at a funeral (some verses are not proper to sing anywhere), and the listeners were shocked that anyone would so dishonor the dead.

"It's the witch!" someone whispered. "The witch—the witch—the witch!" echoed through the crowd.

The singing, which seemed to come out of the clear air above the grave, grew louder and more bawdy, and bursts of laughter punctuated the lewd words. The mourners hurried up the hill and into the Bells' home. Then, as soon as they were inside, the singing stopped. The infamous Bell Witch had finished one of her most celebrated performances. And she had carried out her vow to "put John Bell in his grave."

73

It all happened more than one hundred and fifty years ago, but the tales of the Bell Witch are still Tennessee's most famous ghost tales—and its most amazing.

John Bell, victim of the witch's hatred, was an unlikely subject for such a visitation. Born in North Carolina in 1750, he, his wife, and their children moved to Robinson County, Tennessee, in 1804.

Bell bought one thousand acres of land along the Red River, cleared fields, planted orchards, and built a sturdy house for his family. Nearby he built a one-room school where his children (Jesse, John, Drewry, Benjamin, Zadoc, Richard Williams, Joel Egbert, Esther, and Betsy) and his neighbors' children were educated.

John Bell was a very religious man. Neighbors said his life was guided by the Bible and by the American Constitution with the most emphasis, of course, on the Bible. He had family prayers (kneeling) three times daily, and his house served as a gathering place for prayer meetings and other worship services.

On those occasions when he had business in town, he was an imposing figure in his long blue split-bottom coat trimmed with silver buttons, his beaver hat, and his linen stock. His fervent political speeches were credited with helping to win many elections, and he never hesitated to speak out for what he felt was right.

In short, John Bell became wealthy and influential with a reputation for genial hospitality, personal integrity, and Christian discipleship. There was certainly nothing in his background or in his personality to suggest that he would literally be tormented to death by a witch.

Bell first encountered the witch, as the spirit chose to be called, in the late summer of 1817. He was walking through his corn field, estimating the possible size of his crop, when he saw a strange animal sitting between the rows. The creature, which looked like a dog, stared at Bell in a way that made the man feel uneasy. He shot at it, and the animal disappeared among the thick corn stalks.

The episode would probably not have caused Bell any concern had not similar events followed.

Within the next few days one of Mr. Bell's sons, Drewry, saw a huge bird, much larger than a turkey, perched on a fence. A daughter Betsy, on an outing with the other children, reported seeing a little girl dressed in green swinging on the limb of an oak tree near the house. Dean, the trusted Negro servant, told of meeting a peculiar black dog at a certain spot in the road each night.

It was later, after the disturbances began at the Bell home, that these "sightings" were connected with the witch.

The commotion at the Bell home began with knockings and bangings on the outside walls, always at night. Mr. Bell, the genial host, would go out to greet the visitor who, he assumed, was making the noise, but nobody was ever there. Night after night the bangings continued, and night after night Mr. Bell conducted futile searches for their origin.

Then the noises moved inside the house. The boys, sleeping in an upstairs room, were awakened by a gnawing sound. It sounded, they said, as if a big rat or a squirrel or even a beaver were biting into the wooden legs of their beds. When they lighted a lamp, the noise stopped, but as soon as they put out the light and dozed off to sleep, the racket would commence louder than ever.

Thorough searches, both day and night, never disclosed any trace of an animal in the room. The legs of the beds remained unscarred although the occupants often believed they were in danger of having their beds eaten from under them!

These unexplained noises were only the beginning of the witch's mischief.

The next phase of her campaign of disruption was to snatch the pillows from beneath the heads of the sleeping Bells and, even on the coldest nights, pull the cover off them. No matter how hard the Bells tried to hold onto the warm quilts and coverlets, a force stronger than any of them pulled the bedding off and threw it onto the floor. If they tried wrapping a quilt around themselves, they were spun out of their cocoon and plunked onto the floor with a thud loud enough to arouse the entire household—which it did.

This yanking of pillows and covers did not long satisfy the fiendish witch: she developed into a vicious hair-puller, slapper, and pincher.

One summer night in 1818 little Williams Bell, who was only six or seven at the time, was awakened by having invisible hands grab his hair and jerk it with such force that he feared his head was being pulled off. His frightened screams were drowned out by shrieks from Betsy in her room across the hall. She, too, had felt her hair pulled by rough, unseen hands. It was the beginning of months of torment suffered by the lovely young girl who, with her father, became the major object of the witch's wrath.

John Bell, up to this point, had tried to ignore the supernatural happenings at his home. He did not wish to be ridiculed by his neighbors, he did not want to upset his own family by putting undue emphasis on the strange occurrances, he still hoped to find a logical explanation for the events—and each day he half expected the intruder to depart. However, when the unseen spirit terrified his children and seemed determined to do them physical harm, John Bell sought help from his close friend, James Johnson.

"I know you will find it difficult to believe," John Bell told his friend, "but a demon has taken up residence in our house. I need your help in determining what is causing our trouble."

So James Johnson and his wife spent the night with the Bells. Johnson was a pious man, a lay preacher, and he led the family prayers and hymns before they all retired for the night.

No sooner had the household settled down than the commotion began. That night the spirit demonstrated all her perverse tricks, like a naughty child showing off for visitors. There were knockings, scratchings, gnawings, chairs turned over, chains rattling, covers snatched off, hair pulled, and faces slapped. Nor did the guests escape: the cover was pulled from their bed, and constant bumpings in their room made sleep impossible.

Mr. Johnson became convinced that the deeds were performed by a force which possessed intelligence, and he tried to talk with it. His initial efforts at communication were not successful, but a few months later his theory proved to be correct.

Greatly puzzled by the mystery, Mr. Johnson advised Mr. Bell to make his plight known and to ask other friends to come help with the investigation. From that time until Mr. Bell's death some two years later, the Bell family had a continuous stream of visitors, some neighbors and some from far away. Not one of them was able to rid the house of its hex or to explain the witch's powers.

The visitors, encouraged by Mr. Johnson, tried to entice the witch to talk, to tell what its mission was. After a time it did begin to make a soft whistling sound when spoken to. Then the whistle changed into an indistinct whisper, and finally that whisper grew clear and strong enough to be heard and understood by anyone in the room.

News that the Bell witch could talk created even greater excitement and brought more visitors to the home. Among the visitors none was more famous or more interested in the phenomenon than was General Andrew Jackson, soon to be elected president of the United States.

Jackson was living at his home near Nashville at the time, and when he heard of the cavortings of the witch at the Bell home he determined to go and investigate for himself. He rounded up some of his fun-loving friends to share the trip. They loaded camping equipment and provisions into a wagon (Jackson did not wish to impose on the Bells' hospitality as so many other visitors had done), and the men set out on horseback behind the wagon.

Jackson reined up his horse to call to a friend, "We're off on a witch hunt to John Bell's place. I'll bet you my best fighting cock against a keg of your best whiskey that the witch is a fraud!" And he rode off.

As the caravan neared the Bell home, the wagon suddenly became stuck on the dry, solid ground. No matter how the driver urged the horses or how hard they strained, the wagon would not budge. Its wheels were locked.

Jackson and his friends dismounted and pushed with all their strength, but not an inch did the wagon move. The men removed the wheels to examine them closely, but they found no fault which could account for the stalled wagon.

"It must be the witch," Jackson said, half in jest.

From above the wagon came a caterwauling voice. "All right, General. Go on! I'll talk to you tonight."

The wagon moved easily and quickly toward the Bell home.

Jackson paid his bet—he had found out that the witch was no fraud.

Meanwhile, the witch's conversations increased in frequency and in duration. She enjoyed amazing her listeners with her knowledge of the Bible and of religious matters. She could sing every hymn in the hymnal, could quote any passage in the Bible, and could argue convincingly any question of theology.

She must have been a faithful if unseen attendant at church services, for she would often astound visiting preachers by repeating word for word their prayers, their hymns, their announcements, and their sermons. She was a talented mimic and could copy voices and inflections perfectly.

She particularly liked to mimic James Johnson whom she called "Old Sugar Mouth" because of the "sweet words he says when he prays and preaches."

Perhaps even more amazing than her interest in religion was her custom of reminding guests of events in their past, often happenings that had occurred miles away. In fact, the witch began making nightly reports of all the doings in the community. Many residents, it is said, improved their conduct for fear their misdeeds would be reported publicly by the witch. She seemed to be able to be everywhere, see everything, hear everything and, most dangerous of all, tell everything!

Her religion was only on the surface, however, and did not prevent her from bedeviling Mr. Bell and Betsy unmercifully. She seems to have hated Mr. Bell and to have envied Betsy. The rest of the family she tolerated, and she even had real affection for Mrs. Lucy Bell.

Many examples are recorded of the witch's devotion to Mrs. Bell, but perhaps the most amazing show of concern came during a time when Mrs. Bell was ill with pleurisy. The witch (she was called Kate although nobody ever knew whether the spirit was male or female—the subject of its true identity was one topic the witch refused to discuss) visited Mrs. Bell each morning during her illness and tried to cheer her by singing to her.

One verse from a song sung daily by Kate ended with the words,

> "Troubled like the restless sea,
> Feeble, faint and fearful,
> Plagued with every sore disease,
> How can I be cheerful?"

Neighbors nursing Mrs. Bell never failed to weep at the witch's plaintive, sweet rendition of the sentimental song.

It was during the same illness that Kate, the witch, brought Mrs. Bell a gift of hazelnuts to tempt her appetite.

"Hold out your hands, Lucy, and I will give you a present," the witch's voice instructed.

A shower of hazelnuts fell from the ceiling into Mrs. Bell's outstretched hands. Then, when Mrs. Bell observed that she could not eat the nuts because they were not cracked, their shells were cracked by strong, unseen hands, and then placed carefully on the bed beside Mrs. Bell.

People in the room who witnessed the event looked in vain for openings in the walls or ceiling, but they found no crevice through which the nuts could have come.

A few days later they were equally amazed when a bunch of wild grapes, freshly picked from a swampy thicket, dropped gently on the bed beside Mrs. Bell.

"Eat your grapes, Lucy. They'll make you feel better," the witch instructed.

Mrs. Bell's recovery began almost at once.

But as Mrs. Bell improved, Mr. Bell's health became worse. He complained of a strange affliction. At first he had the sensation of having a stick lodged crossways in his mouth. This was not too upsetting since it occurred infrequently and was of short duration, but as the witch's hatred for him increased, this ailment grew in seriousness.

Mr. Bell's tongue swelled until it filled his whole mouth, making it impossible for him to eat or speak for hours or even days at a time.

In addition, the witch tantalized him in other ways, sometimes snatching off his heavy work shoes, no matter how tightly the laces were tied, and slapping him with such force that his face showed the distinct marks of a handprint and ached for hours.

And all the while Kate boasted that she intended to put John Bell in his grave.

Finally Mr. Bell's afflictions coupled with the constant taunting threats of the witch sent him to his bed where he died on December 20, 1820.

His death, witnesses said, was caused by a potent poison which the witch boasted she had poured between his lips during the night. The poison was never identified (even the doctor called to attend the dying man could not classify it), but when a few drops of liquid from the cloudy vial were placed on the tongue of a cat, the creature whirled around, sprang crazily into the air, keeled over, and died.

And the witch's taunting laughter filled the room.

After the death of John Bell, Kate concentrated her devilment on young Betsy Bell.

Betsy, in her late 'teens, was an unusually pretty girl, taller than average and with a graceful carriage. Her eyes were blue and sparkling, and her flaxen hair was long and quite wavy. She was a bright, intelligent girl, always praised by Professor William Powell for her fine school work, and she had a happy, sunny disposition. Or she had until the witch began tormenting her.

The Bell tombstone at Adams, Tennessee

Betsy and Joshua Gardner, a handsome young man whom she had known since childhood, were deeply in love. Their plans for marriage displeased old Kate, and she alternately pleaded with Betsy not to marry Josh ("Please, Betsy Bell, don't marry Josh") and threatened her with dreadful consequences if she became his wife ("If you marry Josh Gardner, you will both regret it to the ends of your days").

And so on Easter Sunday, 1821, Betsy returned to a heart-broken Josh Gardner the engagement ring she had accepted from him only the day before. He left the community before the week was out, and the lovers never met again.

After a proper interval, Betsy married her former school teacher, William Powell, and the two apparently had a good marriage until his death seventeen years later. In 1875 Betsy moved to Panola County, Mississippi, to live with her daughter, and she died there in 1890 at the age of eighty-six.

With the death of John Bell and the termination of the romance between Betsy and Josh, the witch's evil reign in the Bell household ended.

But descendants of John Bell's family still talk about the strange visitation of the witch and of the turbulant distress she caused.

They call it "Our Family Trouble."

He could not see the sign painted on the side of the long brick building, but he knew what it said: PRATTVILLE COTTON MILL

●●●

The Spirit Of The Spindles

●●●

Willie Youngblood, who was only about ten years old, wanted to stay at home that cold December day (there were kittens in the box behind the kitchen stove), but he had a job in the cotton mill so off to work he went. It was still dark when he left his house, dark and cold, and he ran to help keep warm. He ran because he was scared, too, though he was not exactly sure why he was frightened.

The path was narrow and usually muddy, but this morning the ground was frozen and spewed up. Willie wished it were light enough and that he had time enough to stop and examine the shafts of ice pushing up from the hard ground, but there was not time. There never was time, never time to do the things he wanted to do.

He hurried faster now—he must not be late!—and as he turned the corner, the lights in the big mill beckoned him on. He could not see the sign painted on the side of the long brick building, but he knew what it said: "PRATTVILLE COTTON MILL" in tall letters and, underneath in smaller letters, "Established 1846."

His dinner bucket, the one that had belonged to his papa, bumped against his knee as he hurried along, and Willie thought hungrily of the biscuits with sausage patties and the baked sweet potato rattling around inside. He remembered the first day his mother had handed him that dinner bucket, how she had put her hands on his shoulders and had looked straight into his eyes and said, "Willie, you're the man of the house now. Ten years old is young to be taking on a man's load, but you've got to do it."

She was dressed in black, Willie remembered. He hated the long black dresses she wore, but his mother said it was proper for a widow, even a poor widow, to wear mourning for a year.

"Your papa used to take this dinner bucket to the mill. Now you take it," she had said.

She had not cried, and neither had Willie.

It all seemed a long time ago, and sometimes Willie could not remember what he did and what he thought and how things were before he "took on a man's load."

Willie walked quickly into the mill and climbed the stairs to the third floor, the spinning room where he worked. At first Willie's fingers were so numb from the cold he could not handle the yarn nimbly, and the supervisor shouted abuses at him. Gradually, as his hands became warmer, Willie moved in rhythm with the machinery, almost hypnotized by his monotonous task.

Hours later, when the signal sounded for dinner time, Willie sat down against the wall to eat the food his mother had prepared. Several of his friends, boys about his own age, worked in the spinning room with Willie, and during the noon recess they congregated to talk and to swap food from their dinner buckets. This particular day they talked about how cold it was and speculated on whether or not the mill pond would freeze over. Willie told a story his father had told him of a skating party the young folks in Prattville had one bitterly cold night when the mill pond had iced over. Even Daniel Pratt himself, the man who built the mills and built the town, had come to join in the festivities.

"Wouldn't it be fun!" Willie exclaimed. "I wish I could see somebody ice-skate. Just imagine gliding out across the mill pond. I'd rather do that than anything in the world!"

Looking out the window, the boys saw patches of ice along the edge of the pond, even at midday, and they wondered aloud how they could make ice skates—just in case!

"Let's ask Abner. He'll know," suggested Willie. Abner worked in the card room on the floor below.

Willie stepped to the edge of the elevator shaft and called through the opening.

"Abner! Hey, Abner!"

But before Abner could answer, Willie stumbled and fell through the open shaft.

He died the next day.

A few years after the boy's death, night watchmen at the mill began telling of a strange woman, dressed all in black, whom they sometimes met on their rounds.

"She looks sad," they all agreed, "and she walks along slowly through the mill, looking around like she's hunting somebody special.

"Don't laugh—I seen her as plain as I see you. It gives you the shivers. First time I saw her, I thought to quit my job, but she seemed harmless enough.

"She's been back three or four times. Always gives me a shock to step off the elevator or come up the stairs and see her walking straight and quiet along the rows of machines.

"But she don't bother me, and I don't bother her."

The stories of the watchmen's encounters with the woman in black varied only slightly, and, although many friends scoffed at their reports and suggested the men were looney from being alone too many nights in the sprawling building, they all steadfastly declared they had definitely seen the black-clad visitor.

In the late 1920's the mill began operating a night shift. Most of the operators on that shift had never heard the tales of the visits by the woman in black, so they were completely unprepared when she appeared that summer night. Workers on the third floor, in the spinning room, saw her first. No one witnessed her arrival—she was just suddenly there. She seemed unaware of the presence of the men for she ignored them completely, even when one or two or them approached her to ask politely if they could help her.

"There was a rush of cold air when I got close to her," one of the men reported later. "It wasn't like anything I ever felt before."

Some of the workers left their machines and followed her—keeping back a respectful distance—down to the card room on the next floor.

Here, as she had done in the spinning room, she walked between the rows of machinery, looking at the people but speaking to no one. The routine was repeated on the first floor in the weaving room. She surveyed the situation there, and then she shook her head in a sad way, walked out the door and glided across the surface of the mill pond into the darkness.

Many operators, plain sensible folks not easily deceived, swear they leaned out the windows of that old mill and watched the woman in black glide gracefully across the pond and disappear in the night.

And many of them believe they saw the ghost of Willie Youngblood's mother, come back to look for her little boy.

Mansion, above, and
courtyard, right, at
1140 Royal Street,
the home of Madame Lalaurie
(Photographs courtesy of Nikki Davis)

●●

The Ghost Of The Barefoot Slave

●●

Madame Delphine Lalaurie's dinner for French General LaFayette was the talk of New Orleans, and reporters for the newspapers there could not find enough synonyms for "elegant" to describe the party properly.

But Madame Lalaurie was not satisfied with the "brilliant social success" she had achieved. As their last guest departed, she turned to her husband and said,

"This house is not at all adequate. You will begin at once to build me a mansion suitable for the brilliant entertaining I do."

Dr. Louis Lalaurie nodded in agreement, and early the very next morning he went to downtown New Orleans to consult architects and builders about plans for the mansion his wife wanted.

Dr. Lalaurie was her third husband (the two previous ones, Don Ramon de Lopez and Jean Blanque, had both died), and the couple had been married less than a year. He had no wish to displease his beautiful, willful bride.

Madame Lalaurie had long been famous in New Orleans for her parties, and after she and Dr. Lalaurie moved into their mansion at 1140 Royal Street, her entertaining increased in scope and brilliance. To the drawing rooms, ball rooms, formal parlors, and dining rooms in the French style three-story house came the city's socially elite as well as the artists, writers, musicians, politicians, and gamblers whose talents or conversations amused Madame Lalaurie.

Her beauty, her wit, her charm, and her intellect combined to make her one of New Orleans' most talked about—and envied—women. Her guests counted themselves fortunate, perhaps even blessed, to be included in what were the Gulf Coast's most sophisticated and stimulating social gatherings.

Not one of those guests would have believed their hostess capable of sadistic torture, for not one of them realized she was mad. Some people did wonder occasionally why she never permitted her slaves to join with other blacks in Congo Square for the wild African dances there each weekend. A few friends commented that, except for her imposing mulatto butler, none of Madame Lalaurie's servants was ever seen in public or seen by her house guests.

Scandal first touched Madame Lalaurie when, in 1833, a neighbor on Royal Street reported to police an incident of horror she had witnessed. She had been looking out her window that moonlit night, the woman said, when she saw and heard a little slave girl run screaming from the Lalaurie home. Behind the child, lashing at her with a long bullwhip, ran Madame Lalaurie. The chase continued around the courtyard and back into the house where, the neighbor said, she could still hear the crack of the whip and the cries of pain as the leather thongs tore into the child's flesh.

Then the terrified girl appeared on the roof of the tall house. Even at this height, Madam Lalaurie pursued her and continued the savage beating until the girl leapt to her death on the pavement below the scrolled eaves.

"It was awful—brutal and awful," the woman reported. "To my dying day I will never be able to forget the sounds of that poor child's bare feet running from death, or her screams or the lethal crack of that whip."

The police investigated and found the battered corpse of a young black girl at the bottom of an abandoned well on the Lalaurie property. Madam Lalaurie was given a quick trial, fined, and ordered to turn her slaves over to the sheriff for sale to more humane owners.

It seemed small punishment for the shocking crime, but Madame Lalaurie had been a McCarthy, and the McCarthys were an influential family in New Orleans. They were a helpful family, too, and her relatives purchased the slaves at the public auction (there were few bids for the emaciated creatures) and returned them to her. The affair had little publicity, and, though it provided exciting gossip, it was never, of course, mentioned at the lavish parties Madame Lalaurie continued to give.

About a year later, on the morning of April 10, 1834, the Lalaurie mansion caught fire. Before the volunteer fire department could organize effective action, smoke had filled the house and the flames were spreading.

Madame Lalaurie walked calmly through the swirling smoke, pointing out to neighbors and friends which of her priceless antiques she wanted them to take from the burning house. Among those friends helping to save the furnishings were a judge and an attorney who happened to go to the kitchen (the fire seemed to have started there, and they carried buckets of water to douse it) where they almost stumbled over the cook.

She was chained to the floor.

The two men broke the chain and carried the old woman to safety. Once outside the house, the Negress confessed to police that she had started the fire ("I just couldn't stand it no longer," she moaned), and she told them that other slaves were chained in the attic of the house.

A rescue team was quickly formed. The men smashed their way into the attic where they freed seven slaves who were fastened to the floor with spiked bands around their necks, wrists, and ankles. Scattered about the attic were instruments of torture so sadistic and so inhuman that the rescuers shrank from imagining their use. Those poor miserable slaves knew how the contraptions were used though— they had had personal demonstrations from an expert,

96

Madame Lalaurie.

The crowd which had gathered outside the house was sickened and infuriated when they saw the starving, tortured wretches brought to safety. They waited expectantly (the fire had been put out) for the police to take Madame Lalaurie into custody and haul her off to jail.

Hours passed and nothing happened. Through the windows the crowd could see Madame Lalaurie strolling about the rooms of her fine house, laughing, and showing helpers where to replace her furniture. That sight was too much for the angry crowd. They surged toward the house, determined to mete out their own brand of justice to the smiling torturer.

As the mob reached the steps, a carriage drawn by two dark horses thundered around the corner of the house and careened down the street. Huddled in the back seat was Madame Lalaurie, and driving the vehicle was her mulatto butler. Enraged men grabbed at the carriage and at the horses' harness in a frantic effort to prevent the mad woman's escape, but the coachman-butler beat them back with his long whip. Some people said it was the same whip with which Madame Lalaurie had driven the slave girl to her death.

And so Madame Lalaurie escaped.

Dr. Lalaurie, who had slipped out of the city earlier, had a small boat waiting at a secluded landing, and the two of them sailed north across Lake Pontchartrain to Mandeville. The couple then made their way to Mobile where they boarded a ship for France.

Reports reached New Orleans a few years later that Madame Lalaurie had been gored and trampled to death by a wild boar while she was hunting in southwestern France. One report said that her gun jammed and she tried to beat the vicious animal back with a long whip. The whip somehow coiled itself around her legs, tripping her and impaling her on the tusks of the boar.

The mansion at 1140 Royal Street was occupied by a series of tenants. It served as headquarters for Union officers during the Civil War and afterwards was a gambling house. As the years passed, the structure became a school for girls, a saloon, an apartment house, and a welfare center. Today it is a privately owned apartment building.

Ask in New Orleans for directions to the place, and the reply is invariably,

"Eleven forty Royal Street? Oh, you mean the Haunted House! It's this way - - -"

For ever since the mad mistress of 1140 Royal Street left its premises, the place has been haunted. Tenants, Union officers, gamblers, school girls, bar tenders, and charity workers have all reported hearing, like resurrected echoes in far rooms, the clanking of chains and hoarse voices pleading for mercy.

And many neighbors tell of hearing, late at night, the sound of bare feet running across a stone courtyard, the crack of a whip, and a child's frightened screams.

●●●

A Ghost Who Inspired Poetry

●●●

When Sylvia floated down the stairway that summer afternoon and smiled at the astonished young man on the landing, she had already lived in Panola Hall at Eatonton long enough to have stirred the curiosity of several generations of Georgia residents and to have had a poem written about her.

> "Stand aside and let her pass—
> Little room she takes, alas!
> Sylvia died, they tell me so,
> Died a hundred years ago."

Author of those lines was Mrs. Louise Reid Pruden Hunt of Eatonton who with her husband, Dr. Benjamin W. Hunt, lived in the massive home called Panola Hall.

Mr. Nelson, the young man on the stair that afternoon, had never heard those poetic lines nor had he ever heard of Sylvia. He was, in fact, a serious-minded, rather prosaic though quite wealthy businessman, not at all the kind of person who would be inclined to believe in ghosts. He had come from Ohio in the interest of establishing a cooperative dairy in Putnam County, Georgia (Eatonton being the county seat). He knew of Dr. Hunt's promotion of dairying in the

101

county (Dr. Hunt is credited with bringing the first Jersey cows to Georgia and with building the first silo in the state), and so he had sought out the Eatonton horticulturist-scientist-banker to help him with his plans for the creamery.

Dr. Hunt, a cordial and gracious man, invited Mr. Nelson to be a guest in his home, Panola Hall.

"We rattle around in that big place with just Mrs. Hunt and me there," Dr. Hunt said. "We like to have company to help us fill up those thirteen rooms. Please stay with us while you're in town."

Mr. Nelson accepted the invitation, after he had been assured that his presence would not inconvenience the Hunts. Dr. Hunt, when he issued the invitation, did not warn Mr. Nelson that he and Mrs. Hunt frequently had an uninvited guest in their home, an apparition whom they called Sylvia.

Actually there was no reason for Dr. Hunt to have mentioned Sylvia since it never occurred to him that she, being a very selective spirit, would choose to have an encounter with Mr. Nelson. She, Sylvia, had been in the house ever since Dr. and Mrs. Hunt moved into it about 1870, not long after they were married, and, so far as the Hunts knew, Sylvia had seldom been seen by anyone except the two of them.

They had never been frightened by the appearances of Sylvia, just a bit startled at first, and after a time they accepted rather casually the fact that the ghost of a beautiful young lady lived in an upstairs bedroom at Panola Hall. Mrs. Hall called the room "Sylvia's lair."

"Perhaps," said Dr. Hunt to his wife after their first visits from Sylvia, "it would be best if we did not discuss this matter with outsiders. They might consider us queer. Even with my scientific training I can find no logical explanation for the appearances of what is obviously a ghost. I do not wish to have to try to explain it to anyone else!"

So, though there had been stories about the ghost in Panola Hall for many years, Dr. and Mrs. Hunt did not revive those stories by telling of their visits from the ethereal lady.

Mrs. Hunt, a gentle woman who wrote poetry and played the piano, was pleased to have Sylvia in her home. There was something so romantic about having a ghost, particularly a ghost as charming as Sylvia, she told her husband. And, she pointed out, Panola Hall was the kind of house that needed—even required—a ghost.

This is Panola Hall at Eatonton, Georgia, the kind of house that needs—even requires—a ghost.

It was Mrs. Hunt who named the spirit though she was never able to say just why she chose Sylvia for the name. It was also Mrs. Hunt who immortalized, if that is the proper word to use in connection with a ghost, Sylvia in a poem:

"Sylvia's coming down the stair
Pretty Sylvia, young and fair.
Oft and oft I meet her there,
Smile on lip and rose in hair."

There were other verses, but Mrs. Hunt never showed them to anybody except Dr. Hunt. She read the poem to him while he was grafting a fig tree in their back garden one afternoon. He made almost no comment, but that night at supper he surprised and delighted her by reciting much of the poem from memory.

They both thought Sylvia would be pleased with her poem.

So it was this Sylvia whom Mr. Nelson had met on the stairs. After he stepped aside to let her pass him on the landing that afternoon—he recalled vividly until his dying day the gentle swish of her full skirts and the delicate scent of her perfume—Mr. Nelson went on up to his room where he wrote a note to his family before he came downstairs again. He looked into the living room and then walked out onto the broad front porch hoping to find the young lady. He was disappointed when he did not see her and when the Hunts did not mention her. Perhaps, he told himself, she will join us at supper. But when they went into the dining room, only three places were set at the table.

Mr. Nelson did not wish to appear rude, but his curiosity compelled him to ask, "Tell me, please, who was the young lady I met on the stair this afternoon? She had on a white dress, and there was a rose in her dark hair."

Dr. and Mrs. Hunt stared at each other. It was a full minute before Dr. Hunt replied.

104

"You met Sylvia, the ghost of Panola Hall."

And then the Hunts told him about Sylvia.

Mrs. Hunt, at the suggestion of her husband, brought out her poem and read it to Mr. Nelson. He was so delighted with the poetry that he requested a copy and, according to friends of the families, he carried the poem with him constantly and was even buried with the verses clasped in his hand.

Accounts of Mr. Nelson's meeting with Sylvia created quite a stir in Eatonton for awhile, but Dr. and Mrs. Hunt were so reluctant to talk about Sylvia (they apparently wished to help her maintain her privacy) that nobody learned much about the ghost beyond the tales they already had heard. Within a few weeks, interest in Sylvia subsided.

It was a good many years later, during the 1920's, that Sylvia again permitted herself to be seen by a stranger. This time it was Eatonton's librarian, Miss Alice Wardwell, who saw her. The library is directly across the street from Panola Hall, back from the street and on a slight elevation. Miss

Through this window Eatonton's librarian, Miss Alice Wardwell, saw Sylvia, the ghost!

Wardwell had been home to supper and had walked back in the twilight to open the library for the evening. It was a hot night and the heat seemed particularly oppressive inside the library, so Miss Wardwell sat outside on the front steps while she waited for patrons. She watched the lightning bugs and listened to the katy-dids and savored the sweetness of the cape jasmine blossoms.

She had sat there on the steps for several minutes when she glanced across the street and saw Dr. and Mrs. Hunt seated in their living room. The shades were raised and the draperies had been pulled back to let in the breeze, so Miss Wardwell had a clear view of the room.

Mrs. Hunt was doing some needlework and Dr. Hunt was reading. It was a peaceful, normal scene except for one thing: there was a young woman standing near Dr. Hunt's chair, and the Hunts were paying her absolutely no attention. Miss Wardwell did not recognize the young lady, but she was amazed that Dr. and Mrs. Hunt would be so rude to a guest. Thoughts of Sylvia came to her mind, but Miss Wardwell dismissed them; the young lady was entirely too real to be a ghost! Yet - - - Miss Wardwell was still watching the scene in the Hunts' living room when several children came to return books to the library.

"Look across the street and tell me what you see," the librarian said to them.

The children turned around and gazed at the Hunts' home. One of the little girls piped up,

"I see Dr. Hunt and Mrs. Hunt in their living room. And there's a pretty lady there. But they aren't talking to her."

Satisfied that she was not "seeing things," Miss Wardwell went into the library with the children.

The next morning Dr. Hunt came over to the library, as he often did, and Miss Waldwell said, in what she hoped was a casual and not a prying tone,

106

"I believe you had a guest last night."

"No," replied Dr. Hunt, "we were alone."

Then Miss Wardwell told him what she and the children had seen. He listened with growing interest and exclaimed,

"Alice, that was Sylvia! We didn't know she was in the room with us last night. So you've seen Sylvia!"

One of Sylvia's last recorded appearances came in 1929, during Mrs. Hunt's final illness. Miss Bessie Butler, a close friend of the family, had come from her home in Madison, Georgia, to be of what help she could during those sad, difficult days. Miss Butler was familiar with the stories about Sylvia, but she did not believe in ghosts, not at all.

Relatives were expected to arrive on the late train, and Miss Butler went upstairs to make sure the guest room, "Sylvia's lair," was in order. She was the only person upstairs: the cook was in the kitchen, and Dr. Hunt and the nurse were with Mrs. Hunt in the downstairs bedroom. Miss Butler smoothed the crocheted bedspread, made sure there was fresh water in the pitcher on the washstand, and picked up a piece of lint from the rug. She was walking over to the window to straighten a curtain when she heard someone tiptoeing behind her. Then a young woman's voice called to her,

"Miss Bessie! Oh, Miss Bessie!"

Miss Butler whirled around and fled from the room, but her departure was not fast enough to prevent her seeing a white blur in the corner.

Downstairs, Dr. Hunt heard Miss Butler running down the steps, and he came out into the hall to inquire what had happened.

"It was Sylvia—upstairs," Miss Butler told him. "I didn't want to see her, but I did. And she tried to talk to me!"

Dr. Hunt was disappointed and provoked that Miss Butler had run away.

108

"Sylvia was trying to give us a message. You should have listened," he said in a sharp voice.

Mrs. Hunt died that night.

Who was Sylvia? Nobody knows. All that is known is that she was young and she was lovely and she appeared to several people—people whom she considered worthy—during her long habitation at Panola Hall.

And in the library across the street from the old mansion (it has been converted into a rooming house now) is a thin volume of verse with a poem that begins,

"Sylvia's coming down the stairs - - -"

●●●

The Defiant Tombstone

●●●

Writing a will is not an easy task, not easy even for a learned lawyer, and Judge John Rowan chose his words carefully. He did not wish to be misunderstood.

"In no case is there to be erected a monument or placed over my grave a tombstone of any kind," the Kentucky lawyer wrote. "In this sentiment I am emphatic and it must not be violated.

"When my venerable and beloved father and mother died, they, like the multitude in that day, were interred without tombstones. My children have been buried in the same way. Neither of them has a tombstone. *Nor will I.* It would be cruel to their memory if I were—my father and mother were more entitled to distinction than I ever was. Besides, there is no distinction among the dead. Pride is an unfit associate of death and the grave.

"I therefore again forbid a monumental stone of any kind."

He read what he had written, made a few minor corrections, and put the document in his desk drawer.

"Surely," he mused, "my family will honor my wishes in this matter." Then he pushed aside morbid thoughts by asking aloud, "I wonder who'll be playing cards at Duncan McLean's Tavern tonight. I'd better go see!"

And he hurried from his law office up the steep slope and around to the stables at the rear of his home, Federal Hill, where a groom had his horse waiting. Not even so important a project as preparing his own will could keep Judge Rowan from the gaming tables long. "In the excitement of cards, I find relief from painful reminiscences," he once confessed to a close friend.

Always, it seemed, tragedy had lurked at John Rowan's elbow. As a child in Pennsylvania he had been so frail that his parents despaired of his life. When it appeared that he would survive, his father decreed that John must be given a fine education since he would never be able to support himself by physical labor.

Accordingly, soon after the American Revolution, William Rowan took young John to Bardstown, Kentucky, and enrolled him in Dr. James Priestly's school there. John was a brilliant scholar, particularly in the classics, and he became so proficient in Latin that he could converse in that language as readily as he could in English, an accomplishment which in later life was to involve him in a duel.

His scholastic brilliance also marked his study of law at Lexington, Kentucky, and by 1795 he had come to the bar in Bardstown. During the early phase of his law practice, Rowan was appointed prosecuting attorney, a prized position for beginners, but this appointment was also destined to bring him unhappiness.

In one of his first appearances in court, he prosecuted a young man on a felony charge, and the man was convicted and imprisoned. The conviction troubled Rowan so deeply that he vowed never again to prosecute but to become a

112

defense attorney. He was almost, he admitted later, tempted to quit the practice of law altogether.

Rowan found partial distraction from his disillusionment by supervising the building of his home on the 1300-acre tract of land which his father-in-law, William Lytle, had deeded to his wife, Ann Lytle Rowan, and to him in 1794. The home was patterned after Independence Hall in Philadelphia, and Thomas Jefferson is said to have been the architect. They named it Federal Hill.

The house stands today, as imposing and splendid as ever, but the thousands of tourists who visit it each year know it not as Federal Hill but as My Old Kentucky Home. For it was here during a visit to his Rowan cousins in 1852 that Stephen Collins Foster wrote his famous song.

Soon after the home was completed, it became a mecca for dignitaries of the early 1800's: Henry Clay, James K. Polk, General Lafayette, James Monroe, and others were entertained in its spacious rooms.

Tragedy came to Federal Hill, too.

The thousands of tourists who visit it each year know it not as Federal Hill but as My Old Kentucky Home.

It was here in February, 1801, that an angry mob surged toward the house, intent on punishing John Rowan for having killed Dr. James Chambers, a surgeon, in a duel. Rowan escaped by dressing his negro servant in his (Rowan's) cape and hat and sending him galloping off on Rowan's horse to decoy the vigilantes while Rowan himself slipped away and hid in nearby cliffs.

The duel between the lawyer and the doctor had its beginning at a card game where the men argued over which of them could converse more learnedly in Latin. In the heated exchange of words (both Latin and English and a few old Anglo-Saxon), Rowan made degrading remarks about Dr. Chambers' wife, witnesses said, and the doctor demanded satisfaction on the field of honor. Later Rowan regretted having spoken in an ungentlemanly way about a woman, and he made a public apology for his behavior, but Dr. Chambers still required that the duel be fought.

For years after the event Rowan relived the horror of firing the shot that killed the doctor and of having his fellow townsmen turn on him in fury. The memory of that duel may have been one of the reminiscences that gambling helped Rowan forget.

Tragedy came again to Federal Hill on July 26, 1833, when four members of the Rowan family died of cholera: Captain William Lytle Rowan, the oldest son, who had stopped at Federal Hill on his way to Washington where he was to have been Secretary of State in President Andrew Jackson's cabinet; Mrs. Eliza Rowan, William's wife; Colonel Atkinson Hill Rowan, the second son, who had just returned from Spain; and Miss Mary Jane Steele, John Rowan's granddaughter. Twenty-six of his slaves also died on that day.

It was a hard memory to erase.

Despite the tragedies, John Rowan became a leader in the developing state of Kentucky. He served seven terms in the legislature, was Secretary of State in Kentucky, was Chief Justice of the Kentucky Court of Appeals, and was elected to the United States Senate.

Rowan had developed from a puny boy into a large, broad-shouldered man six feet one and one-half inches tall. He stood erect but was slightly lame from a stagecoach accident, an infirmity which he resented. His legal acumen, his mastery of language, his addiction to gambling, his inflexible integrity, his proud patriotism, his political prowess, his skill as a duelist were all woven into the character of the man, Judge John Rowan.

So when he died (July 13, 1843) many people felt that the instructions in his will should be ignored and that a fitting marker should be placed on his grave. Furthermore, his daughter maintained that she had received his verbal approval for marking the family graves—including his. But his will was never amended to reflect this change of attitude, a rather unusual oversight—if indeed that is what it was—for a man trained in and dedicated to the legal profession.

Perhaps, his close friends speculated, Judge Rowan really wanted Federal Hill to be his memorial. The massive house, they pointed out, was so close to his burial place that in the late afternoon its long shadows almost reached out to touch the grave.

"Federal Hill," they said, "is monument enough for any man." And they were uneasy somehow when talk continued of plans to erect a marker on the grave. In life few men had dared defy John Rowan, and many of his former associates were fearful of violating his wishes even after his death.

"Better do like Marse John say," servants on the place muttered. "He may be dead—but he ain't helpless!"

But despite reminders of the explicit instructions in Judge Rowan's will and despite warnings that he, even in death, might not react kindly to having his orders ignored,

115

plans were completed for erecting an imposing marker at his grave. There is no record of the date the heavy shaft was set in place, nor is there any account of ceremonies attendant upon the event. Even the name of the stonecutter who carved on the face of the marker a listing of John Rowan's public achievements and an assessment of his personal character has been forgotten.

Nonetheless, the story persists that shortly after the memorial had been placed in the small graveyard, it toppled to the ground.

Members of the family did not wish to have a fresh flurry of talk about the controversial marker, so they hastily summoned stonemasons to replace it before accounts of its mysterious fall spread through the town. These craftsmen, long experienced in fostering man's effort to prolong his earthly ties with chiseled words on cold stone, had no explanation for the collapse of the column. They talked vaguely of the ground settling and of tree roots undermining the foundations, but even they appeared unconvinced by such theories.

They, the stonemasons, worked rapidly with hoists and levels and mortar to set the stone shaft firmly in place again. Once the marker was solidly upright, the workmen gathered up their tools and walked rapidly away from the scene as if they half expected to hear behind them the dull thud of heavy stone tumbling to earth. The silence was reassuring— and welcome.

Several weeks or possibly months later, however, the stonemasons received word that their services were required again at the Rowan cemetery: Judge Rowan's marker had fallen from its base. Some of the men refused to return to the cemetery.

"Judge Rowan said he didn't want a marker on his grave—and it looks like he meant what he said," one of the

116

men declared. Others shook their heads and said they wanted nothing to do with a tombstone that would not stay put.

The workers who did go back to the graveyard were even more puzzled by the second toppling of Judge Rowan's stone than they had been when it first happened.

"There's no reason—no logical reason—for that monument to fall," they agreed.

And though they did not say so out loud, they also agreed that old Judge John Rowan likely had something to do with the strange occurrance.

Judge Rowan generally meant what he said, and he had said,

"I forbid a monumental stone of any kind—"

Judge Rowan's Monument at Bardstown, Kentucky

●●

An Eternal Embrace

●●

Colorful pamphlets from Florida's Silver Springs urge, "Explore the indescribable beauty of the world's largest group of crystal clear springs through the magic of glass bottom boats . . ."

Most visitors to this tourist attraction do ride in the glass bottom boats, and most of them, during that ride, hear the tragic story of the young lovers who, in death, created the legend of the Bridal Chamber.

People still living near Silver Springs remember Aunt Silla, the ancient black who seemed as ageless and as immortal as the very springs themselves. It was she who told the stories of the lovers, she who knew them both.

Theirs was the classic story: the rich boy, Claire Douglass, in love with the poor girl, Bernice Mayo.

The way Aunt Silla told it, she had known and loved Bernice Mayo since the girl was a blonde toddler. Bernice was one of a houseful of children of Tom and Jessie Lee Mayo, sharecroppers on the land owned by Captain Harding Douglass. During the summer that Bernice was two, that fateful second summer when so many babies used to sicken and die,

119

she was stricken with an illness for which her parents could find no cure. Always a frail child, Bernice lost her appetite, became listless, and had fever so high that her thin body was almost scorching to the touch. The Mayos had no money to pay a doctor, and when they walked up to the big house and asked Captain Douglass for money for a doctor, he cursed them and ordered them off his porch. So they tried again all the home remedies they knew and watched with sad hearts as their little girl grew weaker and weaker.

One day Aunt Silla, who lived in a cabin on the shores of Silver Springs, passed the Mayos' house on her way to town. She saw Bernice lying on a quilt on the edge of the porch, and she stopped to inquire about the child. She listened quietly as Mrs. Mayo told the long story of Bernice's illness. When the story ended, Mrs. Mayo was weeping, and Silla herself found it hard to hold back the tears.

"Don't cry," she said to Mrs. Mayo. "Crying ain't gonna help." She paused a minute, looked at the sick child, and said, "I believe I can make her well. There are some roots and herbs that grow in the woods near my cabin—they'll cure her. If you'll let me take her home with me, I'll nurse her back to health."

Mr. and Mrs. Mayo agreed to let Aunt Silla take Bernice home with her, so the woman gathered the limp baby up in her arms and returned to her cabin. Three weeks later, Bernice, rosy and strong, ran laughing into the outstretched arms of her mother.

Thus began a friendship between Aunt Silla and Bernice that deepened through the years. Aunt Silla, watching Bernice grow up, gloried in her beauty and in her gentleness. Often they would sit outside Aunt Silla's cabin while the old woman brushed Bernice's long blonde hair and talked about what the future held for her.

"Don't you worry, child," Aunt Silla would say, "you

120

won't always be poor. Some day a rich young man will fall in love with you. He'll be handsome, too," and she would weave a romantic story, ending with, "And old Aunt Silla will come nurse all your children!"

Although she never mentioned him to Bernice, Aunt Silla had a particular young man in mind when she told the stories. The lover she had selected for Bernice was Claire Douglass, only son of the man who owned the fertile acres from which Bernice's father tried to grub a living.

Claire was nothing like his harsh, tyrannical father. He was a sensitive young man, much like his mother who, years before, had fled from the domineering Captain Douglass. Claire could scarcely remember his mother, and Captain Douglass had forbidden anyone on the place to mention her name. The only reminder Claire had of her was a narrow gold bracelet set with pearls and rubies. She had smuggled it to him years before with a note saying, "Remember, I love you always—Mother."

Captain Douglass and Claire never understood each other, and as Claire grew older their quarrels became more bitter. It was after a violent argument with his father that Claire sought out the peaceful solitude of Silver Springs to calm his temper and clear his mind.

As he sat beside the spring, he heard a twig snap behind him and turned to see a young girl running through the trees. Claire sprang up and ran after her, wondering if perhaps his senses had played a trick on him for he had never seen such a lovely girl before.

He was about to give up the chase, convinced that it was a trick of imagination and not a real girl he had seen, when he came to a clearing in the woods and saw the blonde nymph laughing and talking with an old Negro woman. Claire approached the pair cautiously for he still did not entirely trust his senses. They greeted him courteously, and in a few

121

minutes the three were engaged in friendly, carefree conversation. Aunt Silla smiled to herself as she saw how happy Claire and her beloved Bernice were together.

That first chance meeting led to many more as the couple's friendship developed into love. They met often at Aunt Silla's cabin, and they borrowed her boat to row out into the clear waters of Silver Springs. They would sit in the boat for hours, watching the springs and dreaming. Of all the springs, they liked the cold, restless Boiling Spring best, perhaps because it symbolized the turbulance in their own lives.

It was while they were watching the Boiling Spring one day that Claire asked Bernice to marry him and she accepted his proposal. He had no ring to give her, but he took from his pocket his mother's jeweled bracelet and slipped it on her arm.

Meantime, Captain Douglass had learned of the love affair, of the trysts, and of the plans for marriage. He was not pleased.

"No son of mine will marry poor white trash," he stormed.

Despite Claire's protests, he was shipped off to Europe in company of a maiden aunt. Before he left, Claire managed to have a final meeting with Bernice to assure her that he would always love her, that he would write every day, and that he would return soon to claim her as his bride.

Captain Douglass prolonged Claire's stay abroad, and he intercepted all the letters Claire and Bernice wrote to each other. Months passed, and Bernice had no word from Claire. "He has forgotten me," she thought. She began to grow listless and to waste away just as she had done during the summer of her babyhood. This time, however, Aunt Silla had no roots or herbs to work a magic cure. She watched helplessly as death came to claim her "honey child."

Bernice knew she was dying—she had no will to live—and she chose to die at Aunt Silla's cabin, near the spring where she and Claire had shared so many happy hours. Before she died, Bernice made Aunt Silla promise to bury her not in the dark earth but in the clear water of Silver Springs.

"You must take my body," Bernice instructed, "to Boiling Spring and put it in the water there. If you love me, you will carry out my wish. Please, dear Aunt Silla - - -"

Aunt Silla wept as she prepared Bernice's body for its watery grave. She brushed the girl's long hair, smoothed her dress, and, in the stillness of the night, placed the body gently in her boat. Slowly she paddled to the Boiling Spring and there, sobbing a prayer, she lowered Bernice's body over into the water.

The next day Claire returned from his long journey. Not once had he heard from Bernice though he had written to her daily for months. She, he assumed, had wearied of waiting for him and had given her love to someone else. His father professed to know nothing of Bernice (he did not mention having made her family move out of their sharecropper house). He did spend much time telling Claire about a lovely young girl, daughter of a rich banker, who was visiting in the neighborhood.

Claire, disturbed and sad, went to Aunt Silla's cabin hoping to learn something about Bernice, but the old woman was not at home. A few minutes later he saw her sitting on the bank of the springs and he hurried toward her. She did not respond when Claire greeted her, and he assumed that she had become senile, a victim of the ravages of age. He could not know that she was lost in deep grief.

Although she did not seem aware of his presence, Claire asked her permission before taking her boat and rowing out toward Boiling Spring. He wanted, once again, to visit the spot where he and Bernice had pledged their love to each other. Then he would do as his father wished and go meet the young lady Captain Douglass had chosen for him to marry.

A kaleidoscope of memories engulfed Claire as he reached the spring, and in each memory he saw Bernice's face, heard her laughter. In the midst of his reverie, he glanced down into the crystal water and, to his horror, saw a woman's hand thrust out of a rock crevice eighty feet below him.

On the wrist was a jeweled bracelet, the bracelet he had given Bernice.

Claire dived from the boat into the sparkling water, down, down, down. He tried to lift the body and return it to the surface, but it was lodged in the rocks, and he could not pull it free. So the bereaved young man clasped Bernice's body to him, holding it in an embrace that has become immortal.

Aunt Silla said the rocks opened up to receive the lovers, then closed again forever.

People who heard the strange story from Aunt Silla knew she spoke the truth. Boiling Spring was renamed the Bridal Chamber, and guides at Silver Springs today tell the story of the lovers' eternal embrace.

And sometimes tourists peering into the seething spring catch glimpses of a young girl and a young man locked in each others' arms. Perhaps it is only shadows they see or reflections in the water, but many of them are certain that they see, quite distinctly, a jeweled bracelet sparkling in the water of the Bridal Chamber.

The bridal chamber (Photograph courtesy of Florida's Silver Springs)

124

Jeffrey, right, with his live female companion

A Final Note

Frankly, until we read Kathryn's stories and saw the photograph of Jeffrey (shown on opposite page) we were skeptical about ghosts. We also were skeptical about ghost books. If anyone besides our reliable and reputable author, Kathryn Tucker Windham, had brought us this photograph, our skepticism would have continued to be spirited, shall we say. Kathryn has been writing for us since her first edition of *Treasured Alabama Recipes* in 1964, and we have come to know her as an earthy and trustworthy friend. So when she maintained, with an eager and genuine south-Alabama expression, that she now owned a house ghost and that here was a photograph of him or her or it, well we borrowed the photograph and asked permission to give it the "third degree."

We began by requesting a reputable art consultant, the Ludwig Studios of Cherry Hill, New Jersey, to give the photograph a controlled and detailed study. Ludwig's photography staff spent several months analyzing Jeffrey by means of technical tests. They performed a series of actual experiments to see if darkroom shenanigans in the first place could have transposed Jeffrey's photograph onto the negative. All to no avail. They could not conjure up an artificial Jeffrey no matter how many photographic tricks they tried. Jeffrey remained not only unsurpassed—he remained unduplicated.

Next we checked out the girl photographed with Jeffrey. Her name is Nikki Davis, and she is a staff photographer for the *Selma Times-Journal* in Selma, Alabama. From a small farming community in Mississippi, she too has a reputation for integrity and honesty. She is photographed with Jeffrey because she, along with several friends, was visiting her newspaper coworker Kathryn Windham one evening when they decided to make photographs in Kathryn's house. They shot two rolls of films that evening. The next day Nikki was developing them casually at the *Selma Times-Journal* when suddenly, Nikki says, "I almost overturned the developing tank." One of the negatives she was developing showed a ghost!

The ghost, Jeffrey, took up residence at the Windham home in Selma about five years ago. The family first became aware of his presence when they would hear someone moving around in the living room or clumping down the hall. But nobody was ever there.

Jeffrey usually confines his activities to stomping up and down the hall, stirring around in the living room, shaking lamps, and setting empty chairs to rocking; but on at least two occasions he has moved objects.

The first thing he moved was a heavy chest of drawers which he shoved three or four inches alongside a wall until the chest blocked the door. That door, which was closed at the time, is the only entrance into the room, and it could not be opened until the barricading chest was moved by pushing with great force against the door.

That same week a cake baked for a friend was placed on the dining table while a hurried search for car keys was underway. During the search for the keys, which lasted only about three minutes, Jeffrey moved the cake over on the table so that it was about to fall onto the floor. One more small push would have upset its balance and spilled it. Nobody was in the house at the time except the cake maker—and Jeffrey.

Then one night, when Jeffrey had not given evidence of his presence for several weeks, some young people had been playing with a ouija board and making a table talk. The conversation, naturally, included references to Jeffrey. During the evening the group took several pictures of one another, using standard film and flash equipment. Next day when the pictures were developed and printed, there was Jeffrey.

THE STRODE PUBLISHERS

Afterword to the Commemorative Edition

In the mid-1960s—maybe because she had publishing friends in north Alabama, or maybe because she thought it would sell and she sure could use the money, or maybe just because she wanted to see if she was up to the challenge—Mother decided she would write a cookbook. *Treasured Alabama Recipes* became an instant big seller, largely because of the stories that accompanied the family collection of recipes.

Shortly after the release of the cookbook, Margaret Gillis Figh, one of Mother's college English professors, called her. "Kathryn, you are going to write another book, and this time it doesn't need to have any recipes in it. It needs to be a book of stories," Dr. Figh told her. "I'll be your collaborator if you like."

About this same time unexplained occurrences began in our house.

I was the only child still at home, my older sister and brother by then off at college. One afternoon Mother and I were in the kitchen rolling out cookie dough. Our house was small but big enough. The narrow kitchen immediately adjoined the small dining room, which opened through paned double doors into the living room.

That afternoon is indelibly imprinted in my memory. I'd floured the rolling pin and Mother had dampened the counter so the edges of the waxed paper wouldn't roll up. We'd sprinkled more flour on the waxed paper—when making cookies nothing should stick to anything else—and the lump of dough was plopped down and ready to roll out.

At that very moment we heard a ruckus in the living room unlike anything I've ever heard since: loud and scratching noises that seemed to come from not one particular area of the room, but rather from a room filled completely with the unsettling sound as though the midget demons of hell might have been turned loose all at once.

We looked at each other, startled, and moved to investigate. Mother wiped flour on her apron as she hurried to open the double doors into the living room. At the first movement of the doors the room became totally silent—no, eerily silent. I was right beside my mother, looking through the panes into the room. "What was that, Mama?" I asked her more out of curiosity than fear. She hesitated. "I have no earthly idea," she said finally.

We stood there for a minute before Mother dismissed it as a squirrel that might have fallen down into the fireplace, though there was no squirrel. There was nothing in that room except the furniture. We went back into the kitchen. As soon as the dough was almost thin enough to make acceptably crisp cookies, it began again, this time louder and with more force than before. And again, the minute Mother pushed the door, it all stopped. Not one item in the room was disturbed. Not one picture was crooked. Not one glass paperweight had fallen from the mantel.

Though Mother and I waited with some anticipation, the remainder of that day was quiet, ordinary. But in the weeks and months that followed, the unaccountable goings-on continued. They began with loud footsteps clumping down the hall, the steps ending abruptly just inside my brother's bedroom with a jarring slam of the door.

Subsequent strangeness took the form of furniture rearranging, not just shifting a bit as it would if a foundation was settling, but honest-to-goodness interior redecorating—beds rearranged to balance dressers moved from one wall to another. Freshly baked cakes flying—not falling, but *sailing*—off the dining room table. We were amazed, entertained, puzzled, but we were never frightened. My brother and sister pooh-poo-hed our stories on their first visits home from college. But as the unusual goings-on manifested themselves to my siblings, they, too, were intrigued.

DILCY WINDHAM HILLEY

⌒

My mother was a multifaceted woman.

She taught a Sunday school class and made sure we went to church twice on the Sabbath. She was a believer.

She also was generous, perhaps to a fault. One Christmas we got extra stockings. As always, we drove down later to my grandmother's house in Thomasville, but Mother made an unexpected detour down a dirt road that she chose at random. We saw an African American woman walking with two small children. They were total strangers to us.

Mother stopped the car and asked me to give the children our extra stockings that were filled with candy, toys, and fruit. The children's mother's eyes sparkled.

"Santa Claus has come for you at the store and now he's come here," she told the children.

That was so like Mother. She told me about visiting a poor family with her father, who was a country banker, when she was young. She played in the dirt with the family's children that afternoon, and later she and her father shared in their meager evening meal.

"You're not better than they are," her father told her when they left. "You're just used to better things." She remembered the lesson all her life.

On the other hand, she believed in the supernatural.

I was skeptical of Jeffrey and her stories. Whenever someone asked me if I believed, my stock reply was, "Sure! Jeffrey sent me to college."

131

That always drew a laugh from the visitor and a wry smile from Mother.

One day, I was preparing to leave Selma for a job in New Mexico. My suitcase was packed and on my bed. Knowing that I had a long way to drive and that it would be many months before I saw Mother again, I embraced her in a lengthy good-bye hug.

Suddenly, my suitcase jumped from my bed, flipped over twice in the air, and landed beside me.

Mother and I just stared at each other.

"Jeffrey," she finally whispered. She wore the same wry smile.

I hit the road quickly. After that, I, too, was a believer.

BEN WINDHAM